Class Trip

Translated by
Linda Coverdale

Metropolitan Books

Henry Holt and Company
New York

Class Trip

A NOVEL

Emmanuel Carrère

Metropolitan Books
Henry Holt and Company, Inc.
Publishers since 1866
115 West 18th Street
New York, New York 10011

Metropolitan Books™ is an imprint of
Henry Holt and Company, Inc.

Originally published in France in 1995 under the title
La Classe de neige by P.O.L.
At the publisher's suggestion, one chapter of the original text
has been cut for the American edition.

Library of Congress Cataloging-in-Publication Data
Carrère, Emmanuel.
[Classe de neige. English]
Class trip: a novel / Emmanuel Carrère; translated by
Linda Coverdale.
p.   cm.
I. Coverdale, Linda.   II. Title.
PQ2663.A7678C4313   1997   96-41696
843'.914—dc20   CIP

ISBN 0-8050-4694-1

Henry Holt books are available for special promotions and premiums.
For details contact: Director, Special Markets.

First American Edition—1997

Designed by Kate Nichols

Printed in the United States of America
All first editions are printed on acid-free paper. ∞

3   5   7   9   10   8   6   4   2

Class Trip

1

FOR A LONG TIME AFTERWARD—EVEN NOW—NICOLAS
tried to remember the last words his father spoke to him. His
father had said good-bye at the front door of the chalet,
telling him once again to be careful, but Nicolas had been
so embarrassed by his presence, so eager for him to leave, that
he hadn't listened. Convinced that everyone was laughing at
them, he had hung his head resentfully, avoiding his father's
parting kiss. At home he would have been scolded for such
behavior, but he knew that here, in public, his father
wouldn't dare.

Surely they had talked earlier, in the car. Sitting in the
back, Nicolas had found it hard to make himself heard above
the noise of the defroster going full blast to keep the windows
clear. He had been anxious to find out if there would be any

Shell stations along the way. Nothing on earth would have made him let his father buy gas anywhere else that winter, because Shell was giving out coupons you could trade in for a Visible Man, a plastic model whose whole front lifted up like the cover of a box, revealing a skeleton and internal organs you could remove and put back again, thus learning about human anatomy. The previous summer, Fina stations had offered air mattresses and inflatable boats; elsewhere the premiums had been comic books, of which Nicolas had a complete collection. He felt lucky, at least in this respect, since his father drove a great deal on his job and had to fill the tank every few days. Whenever his father went on the road, Nicolas asked to be shown the route on a map so that he could calculate the number of miles and convert it into coupons, which he stashed in a safe the size of a cigar box, with a combination known only to him. It was a Christmas present from his parents ("For your little secrets," his father had said), and he had insisted on bringing it along in his bag. He would have really liked to count up his coupons during the trip and figure out how many he still needed, but his bag was in the trunk and his father had refused to pull over, saying that they'd get it when they stopped for gas somewhere. In the end, there had been no Shell stations or any other reason to stop before they reached the chalet. Seeing how disappointed Nicolas was, his father had promised to drive enough between then and the end of ski school to win the plastic model. If Nicolas would entrust him with all his coupons, it would be waiting for him when he came home.

The last stretch of the trip had taken them along minor roads that had too little snow to warrant putting chains on the tires—another letdown for Nicolas. Before that, they'd been driving on the highway. At one point, the traffic had slowed, then come to a standstill for a few minutes. Nicolas's father had drummed his fingers on the steering wheel in frustration, grumbling that this wasn't normal for a weekday in February. From the backseat, Nicolas could see only a hint of a profile above the thick neck tightly encircled by the overcoat collar. The profile and the neck betrayed anxiety, and a bitter, thwarted rage. At last the cars began to move again. Nicolas's father sighed, relaxing a little bit. Probably just an accident, he said. Nicolas was shocked by the relief in his voice: as if an accident—since it would create a traffic jam only until help arrived—could be considered something desirable. He was shocked but also intrigued. Glued to the side window, he hoped to see crumpled metal, bloodied bodies carried away on stretchers in the glare of flashing lights, but he saw nothing, and his father, surprised, remarked that no, it must have been something else after all. The bottleneck gone, its mystery remained.

2

THE CLASS HAD LEFT FOR SKI SCHOOL THE DAY BEFORE, by bus. Ten days earlier, however, there had been a tragic accident, pictures of which had been shown on the news: a large truck had crashed into a school bus, and several children had died horribly in the flames. A meeting was held the next day at school to prepare for the class trip. Parents were to receive final instructions concerning their children's belongings: what clothes were to be marked; the stamped envelopes to be provided for letters home; the phone calls, on the other hand, that were best avoided (except in an emergency), to help the boys feel truly off on their own, not tied by a thread to their families. Several mothers were distressed by this last instruction: the children were so young . . . Patiently the teacher repeated that it was in their interest. The main purpose of such a trip was to teach them how to stand on their own two feet.

Nicolas's father remarked, rather brusquely, that the main purpose of school was not, in his opinion, to cut children off from their families and that he wouldn't hesitate to call if he felt like it. The teacher opened her mouth to reply, but he pressed on. He had come to raise a much more serious question: the safety of the bus. How could they be sure there wouldn't be a catastrophe like the one they'd all seen recently on the news? Yes, how could they be sure, chimed in other parents, who'd doubtless been wondering the same thing without daring to raise the issue. The teacher admitted that, unfortunately, there was no way to be sure. She could only say that they were taking every precaution with regard to safety, that the bus driver was extremely reliable, and that reasonable risks were a part of life. If parents wanted to be absolutely certain that their children wouldn't be hit by cars, they'd have to prevent them from ever leaving home— and that wouldn't keep them from having accidents with household appliances or from simply getting sick. Some parents conceded the soundness of this argument, but many were shocked by the teacher's fatalistic attitude. She was even smiling as she spoke.

"It's easy to see they're not your children!" exclaimed Nicolas's father. No longer smiling, the teacher replied that she had a child, too, and that he'd taken the bus to ski school the year before. Then Nicolas's father announced that he preferred to drive his son to the chalet himself: at least that way he'd know who was behind the wheel.

The teacher pointed out that the chalet was almost three hundred miles away.

So what? He was determined to make the trip.

But it wouldn't be good for Nicolas, she insisted. Wouldn't help him fit into the group.

"He'll fit in just fine," said his father, and he laughed sarcastically. "Don't try to make me believe arriving in a car with his dad will make him an outcast!"

The teacher asked him to think it over carefully, suggested that he speak with the school psychologist (who would confirm her opinion), but admitted that the final decision was up to him.

In school the next day, the teacher attempted to talk to Nicolas about this, to find out whose idea it was. Treading carefully, as she always did with him, she asked what he would prefer. The question made Nicolas uneasy. Deep down, he knew perfectly well he'd rather travel on the bus like everyone else. But his father had made up his mind, he wouldn't change it, and Nicolas didn't want the teacher and the other boys to think he was being forced to go along with his father's wishes. He shrugged, said he didn't care one way or the other—it was okay the way it was. The teacher left it at that. She had done what she could, and since she clearly couldn't change anything, it was better not to make a fuss.

3

NICOLAS AND HIS FATHER REACHED THE CHALET SHORTLY before nightfall. The other boys, who'd arrived the previous day, had taken their first skiing lesson that morning and were now in the main room, on the ground floor, watching a film on alpine flora and fauna. This was interrupted by the arrival of the newcomers. While the teacher greeted Nicolas's father out in the hall and introduced him to the two instructors, the children in the room began to make a commotion. Nicolas watched from the doorway without daring to join them. He heard his father ask how the skiing was going and an instructor reply laughingly that there wasn't much snow, the kids were learning mostly how to ski on grass, but it was a start. Then his father wanted to know if they'd receive a certificate at the end of the course. An intermediate's star? The instructor chuckled again and said, "A beginner's snowflake, perhaps." Nicolas stood shifting from one foot to the other, his face impassive. When his father finally was ready to leave, Nicolas grudgingly allowed himself to be kissed but did not go outside to see his father off. From the hall, he listened with relief to the motor rumbling out on the driveway, then moving off into the distance.

The teacher sent the instructors to restore order and start the film rolling again while she helped Nicolas settle in. She asked him where his bag was, intending to carry it upstairs. Nicolas looked around; there was no bag to be seen. He didn't understand.

"I thought it was here," he mumbled.

"You're sure you brought it with you?" asked the teacher.

Yes, Nicolas definitely remembered that they'd put it in the trunk, between the tire chains and his father's sample cases.

"And when you arrived, you took it out of the trunk?"

Biting his lips, Nicolas shook his head. He wasn't sure about that. Or rather, yes: now he was certain that they'd forgotten to remove it. They'd stepped out of the car, later his father had gotten back in, and they hadn't ever opened the trunk.

"How silly," said the teacher, not at all pleased. The car had left barely five minutes before, but it was already too late to catch up with it. Nicolas felt like crying. He stammered that it wasn't his fault. "You could have at least thought of it," sighed the teacher. Relenting when she saw how miserable he looked, she shrugged and said it was a silly mistake but not a serious one. They'd figure something out. Anyway, his father would quickly realize what had happened. Yes, agreed Nicolas: when he opened the trunk to get his sample cases. Hearing this, the teacher was confident he'd soon return with the bag. Yes, yes, said Nicolas, torn between his desire to have his things back and his fear of his father's return.

"Do you know where he's planning to stop for the night?" asked the teacher.

Nicolas didn't know.

Darkness had fallen, making it unlikely that Nicolas's father would show up with the bag before morning. It was therefore necessary to make some arrangement for that night. The teacher and Nicolas returned to the main room, where the film was over and everyone was getting ready to set the table for dinner. Following the teacher through the door, Nicolas felt painfully like the new kid who doesn't know what's going on, the kid everyone makes fun of. He sensed that the teacher was doing what she could to protect him from any teasing or hostility. After clapping for silence, she announced in a joking tone that Nicolas—off in the clouds, as usual—had forgotten his bag. Who would lend him some pajamas?

Since each student's list had specified three pairs, anyone could have lent him some, but nobody spoke up. Not daring to look at the children gathered around them, Nicolas stayed close to the teacher, who repeated her appeal with a touch of irritation. He heard giggles, and then a voice he couldn't identify said something that made the others burst out laughing: "He'll pee in them!"

It was pure meanness, a random shot, but it hit home. Nicolas did still occasionally wet his bed, not very often, but even so he dreaded sleeping anywhere except in his own room at home. From the very start, this had been one of his greatest anxieties about ski school. At first he'd said he didn't want to go. His mother had requested a meeting with the teacher, who had reassured her that he probably wouldn't be the only one, and besides, that kind of problem often disappeared in a group setting. Just in case, it would be a good idea for him to take along one more set of pajamas and a drawsheet to protect the mattress. Despite these comforting words, Nicolas had watched nervously as his bag was packed: since they were going to sleep in dormitories, how could he place the drawsheet over the mattress without anyone noticing? This worrisome thought and a few others like it had tortured him before he left, but even in his worst nightmare he'd never have imagined what was actually happening to him:

finding himself without his bag, the drawsheet, pajamas, reduced to begging in vain for a pair, mocked and stripped naked as soon as he arrived, as though his shame were written all over his face.

Finally, someone said he'd lend him some pajamas. It was Hodkann. That sparked fresh merriment, because he was the tallest boy in the class, while Nicolas was one of the smallest, so the offer almost seemed intended to poke more fun at him. But Hodkann put a stop to the jeers by saying that whoever bothered Nicolas would have to deal with him, and everyone knew he meant it. Nicolas gave him a flustered, grateful look. The teacher seemed relieved but perplexed, as though she suspected a trap. Hodkann had great authority over the other boys, which he exercised in a capricious fashion. In all games, for example, they took their cues from him, without knowing whether he would behave like a referee or a gang leader, dispensing justice or flouting it cynically. Within the space of a few seconds, he could be extraordinarily kind and extraordinarily brutal. He protected and rewarded his vassals but banished them without cause as well, replacing them with others whom he'd previously disdained or mistreated. With Hodkann, you never knew where you stood. He was feared and admired; even adults seemed afraid of him. He was about as tall as an adult, moreover, with a nearly grown-up voice and none of the clumsiness of boys who shoot up too quickly. He moved and spoke with an ease that was almost disconcerting. Although he could be vulgar, at times he expressed himself extremely well, with a richness and precision of vocabulary surprising for his age. He received very good grades or very bad ones, without seeming to care either way. On the form everyone filled out at the beginning of the school year, he'd written, "Father: deceased," and everyone knew he lived alone with his mother. On Saturdays she came to pick him up at noon in a little red sports car. Although she stayed in the car, it was easy to see that she didn't look like the other boys' mothers, with her aggressive, made-up beauty, her hollow cheeks, her mane of red hair that seemed hopelessly tangled. The rest of the week, Hodkann went to and from school on his own, by streetcar. He lived far away, and everybody wondered why he didn't attend a school closer to his home, but this kind of question, which would have been easy to put to someone else, became impossible if you were face-to-face with Hodkann. Watching him head off toward the streetcar stop, his book bag on his shoulder (he was the only one who didn't carry a school satchel strapped to his back), the children tried—each of them secretly, because no one dared talk about him in his absence—to imagine his ride, the neighborhood where he and his mother lived, their apartment, his room. There was something both improbable and mysteriously attractive about the idea that somewhere in the city there existed a place that was Hodkann's room. No one had ever been there, and he himself didn't go to the other boys' homes. He shared this distinction with Nicolas, in whose case, however, it was less peculiar, and Nicolas hoped that no one had noticed it. Nobody ever thought of inviting him or expected to be invited to his home. He was as timid and unobtrusive as Hodkann was bold and self-assertive. Ever since the beginning of the year, he'd been scared to death that Hodkann would notice him, would ask him something, and he'd had several nightmares in which Hodkann had singled him out for bullying. So he was quite worried when Hodkann—in a sudden fit of benevolence, like a Roman emperor in the arena—brought the pajama torture to an end. If Hodkann was taking him under his protection, that meant he might just as easily abandon him or hand him over to others whom he'd already turned against him. Many sought Hodkann's favor, but all knew it was dangerous, and Nicolas had managed not to attract his attention until now. Well, that was over. Thanks to his father he'd attracted everyone's attention, and he felt he'd been right about ski school all along: it was going to be a dreadful ordeal.

4

MOST OF THE STUDENTS ATE IN THE CAFETERIA, BUT NOT Nicolas. His mother came to get him and his younger brother, who was still in nursery school, and the three of them ate lunch at home. The boys' father said that they were very lucky and that it was a shame their classmates had to use the cafeteria, where the food was terrible and fights often broke out. Nicolas agreed with his father and, when asked, declared that he was glad to escape the bad food and the roughhousing. He realized, though, that his classmates formed their strongest bonds between noon and two o'clock, in the cafeteria and on the playground, where they hung around after lunch. While he was gone, they'd thrown yogurts at one another, been punished by the monitors, formed alliances, and each time his mother brought him back it was as if he were a stranger who had to start all over again on the relationships he'd begun forming that morning. He was the only one who remembered them: too many things had happened during that two-hour lunch period.

He knew that the chalet would be like the cafeteria, but lasting two weeks, without a break or the possibility of going home if it turned out to be too hard on him. He was afraid of that, and his parents were too—so much so that they'd asked the doctor if he'd write an excuse for Nicolas. But the doctor had refused, assuring them that the trip would do him a world of good.

In addition to the teacher and the bus driver, who was also in charge of the kitchen, there were two instructors at the chalet, Patrick and Marie-Ange, who assigned teams to set the table after Nicolas had rejoined the other children: some busied themselves with the silverware, others with the plates, and so on. Patrick was the one who had spoken so lightheartedly to Nicolas's father about skiing on the grass. Tall, with broad shoulders, he had a tanned, angular face, very blue eyes, and long hair worn in a ponytail. Marie-Ange, a trifle chubby, revealed a broken front tooth when she smiled. Both wore green-and-purple track suits and little bracelets woven of multicolored threads that you tied on your wrist while making a wish and left on until they fell off by themselves, when your wish—supposedly—had come true. Patrick had a whole supply of these bracelets, which he distributed like medals to children he was pleased with. Just after Nicolas joined the group, he gave him one, which upset several boys who'd been hoping to get them. Nicolas hadn't done anything to deserve his! Instead of saying that poor Nicolas needed to be consoled because he didn't have his things with him, Patrick laughed and told the story of how when he and his sister were little their father always punished one when the other had been naughty, and vice versa, so they would learn early on that life could be unfair. Nicolas thanked him silently for not making him look like a crybaby, and as he went around the tables setting out the soup spoons Patrick had entrusted him with, he thought about the wish he would make. First he considered asking not to wet his bed that night, then asking not to wet his bed the whole time he was in ski school, but he realized that he might as well ask for his entire stay in the chalet to go well. And why not ask for everything to go well for the rest of his life? Why not wish that all his wishes would always come true? The advantage of a wish that was as general as possible, encompassing all specific wishes, seemed so obvious at first glance that he knew there was a catch, something like the story of the three wishes, which he knew in its nice version for children (with a peasant whose nose changes into a sausage) but also in a much grimmer variation.

Above his parents' bed at home was a shelf full of books

and dolls in folk costumes. Most of the books were about herbal healing or do-it-yourself repairs, but two of them fascinated Nicolas. The first, a big green volume, was a medical dictionary that he didn't dare carry off to his room for fear it would be missed, so he had to read it in quick snatches, his heart pounding, while he kept an eye out through the half-open door. The other book was called *Tales of Terror*. The cover showed a woman from the back as she looked into a mirror, and in the mirror you could see a grinning skeleton. This one was a paperback, easier to handle than the dictionary. Without saying anything, figuring that his parents would confiscate the book and tell him he was too young to read it, Nicolas had sneaked it into his room, hiding it behind his own few books. When he lay sprawled across his bed on his tummy, immersed in its pages, he kept ready as a cover in case of emergency his collection of *Tales and Legends of Ancient Egypt*, in which he'd read the story of Isis and Osiris a good ten times. One of the scary stories told how an elderly couple discover the powers of a kind of amulet: the severed paw of a monkey, a shriveled, blackish thing able to grant three wishes to its owner. Without thinking or even really believing in what he's doing, the man asks for a certain sum of money he needs to repair his roof. The woman immediately upbraids him for his foolishness, saying he should have asked for a lot more—he has wasted the wish! A few hours later, there is a knock on the door. It's an employee from the factory where their son works. The man is quite distressed, he has ghastly news for them. An accident. Their son was caught in the gears of a machine and killed, torn to shreds. The manager of the factory would like them to accept some money for the funeral: exactly the amount the father had asked for! The mother howls with grief and now makes her own wish: that their son be given back to them! And so, at nightfall, the scraps of his dismembered body drag themselves to their door, little gobbets of bloody flesh twitching on the front steps while one severed hand tries to get into the house in which the horror-stricken parents have barricaded themselves. They have only one wish left: that this thing without a name should vanish! That it should die once and for all!

5

SIX COULD SLEEP IN EACH BEDROOM, AND THERE WAS one place available in Hodkann's. Without asking anyone's opinion, he announced that Nicolas would take it. The teacher approved: although she was still worried about his sudden mood swings, she liked the idea of the biggest boy in the class looking after the smallest one like this. She felt somewhat sorry for shy, overprotected Nicolas. The rooms were furnished with bunk beds. Since Hodkann had assigned him to an upper bed, above his own, Nicolas climbed the ladder and wriggled into the borrowed pajamas, rolling up the legs and sleeves. The top came down to his knees; the pants swam on him. Going to the toilet, he had to hold the pants up with both hands. And he had no slippers, towel, washcloth, or tooth-brush—things no one could lend him because they didn't have extras. Luckily, nobody paid any attention to him, so he was able to slip unnoticed through the bustling bathroom and be among the first ones in bed. Patrick, who was in charge of his room, came over to muss his hair and tell him not to fret: everything would be fine. And if there was anything wrong, he would come to Patrick and tell him about it, promise? Nicolas promised, divided between the real comfort this assurance gave him and the painful impression that everyone was waiting for something to go wrong for him.

When they were all in bed, Patrick turned out the light, said good night, and closed the door. They were left in the dark. Nicolas thought that a ruckus would break out immediately, a pillow fight in which he'd have trouble holding his own, but no. He realized that everyone was waiting for Hodkann's permission to speak. Hodkann let the silence last for a long while. Gradually their eyes grew accustomed to the gloom. Their breathing became more even, but there was still a feeling of expectation in the air.

"Nicolas," said Hodkann at last, as though they were alone in the room, as though the others didn't exist.

"Yes?" murmured Nicolas, like an echo.

"What does your father do?"

Nicolas replied that he was a traveling salesman. Nicolas was rather proud of this profession, which seemed to him prestigious, even a little mysterious.

"So he travels a lot?" asked Hodkann.

"Yes," said Nicolas, repeating something he'd heard his mother say. "He's on the road all the time."

He was working up the courage to mention the advantages this meant for premiums from gas stations, but he didn't get the chance: Hodkann wanted to know what his father sold, what kind of stuff. To Nicolas's great surprise, Hodkann seemed to be asking questions not to make fun of him but because he was truly curious about what his father did. Nicolas said that he sold surgical supplies.

"Forceps? Scalpels?"

"Yes, and artificial limbs too."

"Wooden legs?" inquired Hodkann in amusement, and Nicolas sensed, like an alarm deep inside him, the threat of mockery closing in.

"No," he said, "plastic ones."

"He drives around with plastic legs in his trunk?"

"Yes, and also arms, hands—"

"Heads?" burst out Lucas, a red-headed boy with glasses whom Nicolas had thought was asleep, like the others.

"No," said Nicolas, "not heads! He's a traveling salesman in surgical supplies, not gags!"

Hodkann greeted this sally with an indulgent chuckle, and Nicolas immediately felt relaxed and gratified. Protected by Hodkann, he, too, could say funny things, make people laugh.

"He's shown you these artificial limbs?" continued Hodkann.

"Of course," said Nicolas, drawing confidence from this initial success.

"You've gotten to try one on?"

"No, you can't do that. Because it goes where your arm or your leg was, so if you've still got your arm or leg there, you've got nowhere to put it."

"Me," said Hodkann calmly, "if I were your father, I'd use you for demonstrations. I'd cut off your arms and legs, I'd fit on the artificial ones, and I'd show you to my clients like that. It'd make a great advertisement."

The occupants of the neighboring bed cracked up. Lucas said something about Captain Hook in *Peter Pan*, and abruptly Nicolas felt afraid, as though Hodkann had finally shown his true face, one even more dangerous than he'd feared. The henchmen, fawning, begin cackling already, while the potentate nonchalantly searches his imagination for the most refined of tortures. . . . But Hodkann, sensing the threat in what he'd just said, removed the sting by saying with that surprising gentleness he sometimes showed, "Don't worry, Nicolas. I'm just teasing." Then he wanted to know if, when

Nicolas's father brought back his bag the next day, they might be able to see those amazing artificial limbs, those sets of surgical instruments. The idea made Nicolas nervous.

"They're not toys, you know. He only shows them to clients . . ."

"He wouldn't show them if we asked him?" persisted Hodkann. "And if you asked him yourself?"

"I don't think so," replied Nicolas in a small voice.

"If you told him that, in exchange, no one would beat you up during ski school?"

Once more apprehensive, Nicolas said nothing.

"Fine," concluded Hodkann. "In that case, I'll find some other way." After a moment, he announced to the room at large, "Time to go to sleep."

They heard him tossing heavily in bed until he found a comfortable position, and everyone knew they shouldn't say another word.

6

ALL WAS QUIET, BUT NICOLAS WASN'T SURE IF THE
others were sleeping. Perhaps—scared of making Hodkann
mad—they were pretending, and maybe Hodkann was as well,
lying in wait for anyone who dared disobey him. As for Nicolas, he didn't want to sleep. He was afraid of peeing in the bed
and wetting Hodkann's pajamas. Or even worse, of peeing
right through the mattress, since there wasn't a drawsheet,
and wetting Hodkann himself below. The smelly liquid would
start dripping down onto his tiger's face, he'd wrinkle his
nose, wake up, and then it would be awful. The only way to
avoid this catastrophe was not to fall asleep. According to the
glowing hands of Nicolas's watch, it was twenty past nine;
wake-up was at seven-thirty, which meant a long night ahead.
But it wasn't the first time: he'd had practice.

The year before, Nicolas's father had taken him and his younger brother to an amusement park. Because of the difference in their ages, the two of them hadn't been interested in the same rides. Nicolas had been most attracted to the Ferris wheel, the haunted house, and the tunnel of terror, while his brother liked the merry-go-rounds for little kids. Their father had suggested compromises and was irritated whenever the children rejected them. At one point, they'd passed a wheel designed to look like a caterpillar turning a circle in the air at top speed. The passengers, clutching the safety bars of their little cars, found themselves hurtling skyward, suspended upside down by centrifugal force. The wheel turned rapidly, faster and faster; you could hear shrieking, and the people got off pale, with wobbly legs, but thrilled by the experience. A boy Nicolas's age remarked excitedly to him that it was cool, and the boy's father, who had gone on the ride with him, gave Nicolas's father a knowing smile to indicate that perhaps it was not so much cool as exhausting. Nicolas wanted to go on the ride, but his father showed him a sign by the ticket window saying that children younger than twelve had to be accompanied. "So come on it with me!" entreated Nicolas. "Oh please, come on it with me!" His father, who did not seem eager to be whirled around head over heels, begged off by pointing out that they couldn't take along his little brother, who'd be petrified, or leave him all alone, unsupervised. Then the father of the boy who'd just gone on the caterpillar kindly offered to watch Nicolas's brother during the three-minute ride. He looked something like an older version of Patrick, the instructor: he was wearing a denim jacket, not a heavy overcoat like Nicolas's father's, and he had a cheerful face. Nicolas gave him a grateful look, then gazed hopefully at his father. But his father told the other man that there was no need to bother. When Nicolas opened his mouth to plead with him, his father shot him a threatening glance and gripped the back of his neck firmly to make him walk on. They moved away from the caterpillar in silence, Nicolas not daring to object while they were still within sight of the other boy and his father. He could imagine their astonished expressions behind his back: why such an abrupt departure in response to a kind offer? When he thought they were far enough away, Nicolas's father stopped and said sternly that when he'd said no, that meant no, and there wasn't any use making a scene in public.

"But why?" protested Nicolas, on the verge of tears. "What difference would it have made?"

"You want me to tell you why?" replied his father, scowling. "You want me to tell you? All right, you're old enough to have it explained to you. Except that you mustn't talk about it, not to your playmates, not to anyone. It's something I learned from the director of a clinic. The doctors all know about it but they don't want it to get around, so as not to frighten people. Not too long ago, in an amusement park like this one, a small boy disappeared. His parents didn't pay attention for a few seconds, and that was that. It all happened very fast—it's quite easy to disappear, you know. They looked for him all day long and that evening they finally found him, unconscious behind a fence. They took him to the hospital— they'd seen there was a big bandage on his back, with blood coming out—and the doctors knew what had happened, they could already tell what they'd see on the X ray: the little boy had been operated on, and one of his kidneys had been taken out. There are people who do that, can you believe it? Bad people. That's called trafficking in organs. They've got vans with everything they need for operations. They prowl around amusement parks or near the entrances to schools, where they kidnap children. The head of the clinic told me they preferred not to spread the information around, but it's happening more and more often. Just in his clinic alone, they've had a kid who had his hand cut off and another who had both eyes ripped out. You understand, now, why I didn't want to hand your little brother over to a stranger?"

After that story, Nicolas had a recurring nightmare that took place in an amusement park. He didn't remember all the details in the morning but sensed that the main thrust of the dream was pushing him toward some nameless horror from which he might never awaken. The metal framework of the caterpillar loomed over the wooden shacks of the park, and the dream was driving him toward it. The horror was lurking over there. It was waiting to devour him. In the second dream, he realized that he'd drawn closer and that the third time would probably kill him. They'd find him dead in his bed: no one would understand what had happened to him. So he decided to stay awake. Of course, he couldn't really manage that; his fitful slumber was disturbed by other nightmares, behind which, he feared, was hiding the one about the park and the caterpillar. He discovered, that summer, that he was afraid to fall asleep.

7

WITHIN THE FAMILY, HOWEVER, IT WAS SAID THAT HE took after his father, who slept badly but a great deal, with a kind of greediness. When he was home for several days in a row after being out on the road, he spent almost all his time in bed. After school, Nicolas would do his homework or play with his little brother, taking care not to make any noise. In the hall, they would walk on tiptoe; their mother was constantly putting her finger to her lips. At dusk, their father would emerge from his room in pajamas, unshaven, his face grumpy and puffy with sleep, his pockets stuffed with crumpled handkerchiefs and empty medicine wrappers. He looked surprised, and disagreeably so, to awaken there, to find these walls pressing in on him, to discover—

pushing open the first door he came upon—a child's bed-room where two small boys, on all fours on the carpet, in-terrupted their game or their reading to look up at him anxiously. He'd manage an uneasy smile, mumbling dis-jointedly about fatigue, lousy schedules, drugs that wiped you out. Sometimes he would sit for a moment on the edge of Nicolas's bed, staring vacantly, rubbing a hand over his raspy beard or through tousled hair still creased from the pil-low. He would sigh, ask strange questions, like what grade Nicolas was in. Nicolas would answer obediently, and his fa-ther would nod, saying that Nicolas was getting into serious schoolwork and should study hard to avoid having to repeat a grade. He seemed to have forgotten that Nicolas had al-ready repeated a grade, the year they moved. One day, he asked Nicolas to come closer, to sit next to him on the bed. He put his hand on the back of his son's neck, squeezing gently. It was to show his affection, but it hurt, and Nicolas twisted his neck cautiously to break free. In a low, hollow voice, his father said, "I love you, Nicolas," which upset the boy, not because he doubted it but because this seemed such a strange way to say it. As though it were the last time before a long—perhaps a final—separation, as though his fa-ther wanted him to remember it his whole life long. A few moments later, though, his father didn't seem to remember it anymore himself. There was a blank look in his eyes; his hands were shaking. Wheezing, he stood up, his burgundy pajamas hanging loosely, all rumpled, and he fumbled his way out, as though he had no idea which door to open to get back to the hall, back to his room, back to bed.

8

NOW NICOLAS WAS THINKING (AND AT LEAST IT WAS helping keep him awake) about Hodkann's declared intention of seeing with his own eyes the samples stored in the car trunk. How would he go about it? Perhaps he'd find a way to stay in the chalet while the others went down to the village for their skiing lesson. Hidden behind a tree, he'd keep his eyes peeled for the car. Nicolas's father would get out, open the trunk to remove the bag, and carry it to the chalet. As soon as his back was turned, Hodkann would rush up, raise the lid of the trunk, then open the black plastic cases containing the artificial limbs and surgical instruments. That was undoubtedly his plan, but he wasn't aware that Nicolas's father always locked the trunk after taking something out of it, even if he knew he was going to be reopening it a few minutes later.

Hodkann was so bold, though, that you could imagine him following Nicolas's father into the chalet and picking his pockets, stealing his key ring while he was speaking to the teacher. Nicolas saw Hodkann bent over the open trunk, forcing the latches of the sample cases, testing the blade of a lancet on the ball of his thumb, bending the joints of a plastic leg, so enthralled that he'd forgotten all danger. Nicolas's father was already leaving the chalet, walking toward the car. Another moment, and he would catch Hodkann. His hand would fall heavily on Hodkann's shoulder, and then—what would happen? Nicolas hadn't any idea. Actually, his father had never threatened dire punishment for touching his samples. Nicolas was certain, however, that even for Hodkann it would be a very tricky situation. The expression "to have a rough time of it" kept running through his head. Yes, if he got caught rummaging through the car trunk, Hodkann would have a rough time of it.

Hodkann's interest in his father bothered Nicolas. He even wondered if the other boy hadn't taken him under his wing to get close to his father, to win his confidence. He remembered that Hodkann didn't have his own father anymore. And when he was alive, this father, what did he do? Nicolas hadn't thought to ask, and anyway, he would never have dared. He couldn't help thinking that Hodkann's father had died violently, in suspicious, tragic circumstances, and that his life had led inexorably to such an end. He imagined him as an outlaw, dangerous, like his son, and maybe Hodkann had become so dangerous only because he had to deal with that, with the risks he ran for being the son of this father. Nicolas would have liked to ask Hodkann about him now. At night, with just the two of them, it would be possible.

It was a voluptuous thought, this nocturnal conversation with Hodkann, and Nicolas spent some time imagining how it would go. They would both leave the room, without awakening anyone. They would talk quietly in the hall or the bathroom. He pictured their whispering, the nearness of Hodkann's big, warm body, and he relished the idea that the tyrannical power wielded by Hodkann concealed a sorrow, a vulnerability that the other boy would confess to him. He would hear him confide, as though to his only friend, the only person he could trust, that he was unhappy, that his father had died gruesomely, dismembered or tossed into a well, that his mother lived in fear of seeing her husband's accomplices reappear some day, determined to avenge themselves on her and her son. Hodkann, so imperious, so mocking, would admit to Nicolas that he was afraid, that he, too, was a lost little boy. Tears coursing down his cheeks, he would lay that proud head on Nicolas's lap, and Nicolas would stroke his hair, speaking gentle words of consolation, consolation for this vast and hitherto unspoken grief that had suddenly burst out before him, for him alone, because only he, Nicolas, was worthy of this revelation. Between sobs, Hodkann would say that the enemies who had killed his father and whom his mother so dreaded might come to the chalet to take him away. To take him hostage or simply kill him, abandoning his corpse in a snowy patch of undergrowth. And Nicolas would realize that it was up to him to protect Hodkann, to find a hiding place where he would be safe when these bad men, who wore shiny dark coats, surrounded the chalet and silently entered, one at each door so that no one could escape. They would draw their knives and strike coldly, methodically, determined to leave no witnesses. The half-naked bodies of children surprised in their sleep would pile up at the foot of the bunk beds. The floor would be streaming with blood. But Nicolas and Hodkann would be hiding in a hollow in the wall, behind a bed. It would be a dark, narrow space, a real rat hole. They would huddle together, their eyes wide with terror and glistening in the shadows. Together they would hear, over the sound of their own breathing, the appalling din of the carnage: shrieks of horror, death agonies, the dull thud of falling bodies, windows shattering into glass shards that would embed themselves in already mutilated flesh, the curt laughter of the killers. The severed head of Lucas, the red-headed boy with glasses, would roll under the bed toward their hiding place, coming to a stop at their feet to stare at them in disbelief. Later, all would be silent. Hours would pass. The murderers would have left empty-handed, exhilarated by the massacre yet seething with vexation at having missed their prey. In the chalet, there would be only corpses, huge heaps of dead children. But the two of them would not leave. They'd spend the whole night crouched in their nook, entrenched in the heart of the slaughterhouse, each one feeling on his cheeks a warm trickling that might be blood from a wound or the other boy's tears. They would stay there, trembling. The night would have no end. Perhaps they would never come out.

9

NICOLAS'S FATHER STILL HAD NOT RETURNED BY THE TIME breakfast was over the next morning. The teacher glanced at her watch. There was no point in waiting around for him and missing the skiing lesson. Nicolas could feel her eyes on him, and for once the look in them was less than indulgent. Perhaps, he said in a small voice, it would be best if he stayed at the chalet. He hoped that Hodkann would volunteer to stay behind as well. "We're not going to leave you all alone," announced the teacher firmly. Patrick observed that nothing much could happen to him, but the teacher said no, it was a matter of principle. In the meantime, she asked Nicolas to go upstairs with her, as she wanted to call his mother to inform her of the situation and find out if she had heard from her husband. The telephone was on the second floor, in a small wood-paneled office with a lovely view of the valley from the window. The teacher dialed the number, waited for a moment, and asked Nicolas in an annoyed tone if his mother usually left home very early in the morning. Nicolas replied contritely that no, she didn't, not usually. Actually, he was glad his mother wasn't answering. This phone call made him uneasy. Few people called them at home; on those rare occasions when the phone did ring, his mother approached it with obvious trepidation, particularly when his father wasn't there. If Nicolas was around, she shut the door so that he wouldn't hear, as though she feared receiving bad news and wished to spare him for as long as possible. The teacher sighed, then redialed the number, just in case she had made a mistake before. This call was answered immediately, and Nicolas wondered what had happened the first time. He imagined his mother in the position in which he had caught her several times: standing in front of the ringing telephone, wincing in dismay, not daring to answer it. When the ringing stopped, she'd seem relieved for a moment, but if the ringing began again, she answered right away, grabbing the receiver the way you'd jump into the water to escape a fire.

Nicolas studied the teacher's face nervously as she introduced herself and explained why she was calling. The phone

was the old-fashioned kind, with an extra earpiece for someone to listen in. Noticing Nicolas watching her, she motioned
for him to pick it up. He obeyed.

"No, " she explained patiently, "it's not serious. But it's in-
convenient. I mean, without his bag he's got no change of
clothes, no ski things, only what he's wearing, so we're not
quite sure what to do with him."

She smiled at Nicolas to take the edge off that last remark,
which had been made largely to provoke a reaction from his
mother.

"But my husband will certainly bring back the bag."

"That's what I'm hoping, but since he hasn't shown up yet,
what I want to know is, where can we reach him?"

"When he's out on the road, he cannot be reached."

"Really? He doesn't know in advance what hotels he'll be
staying in? What happens if you need to talk to him ur-
gently?"

"I'm very sorry. That's just how it is," said Nicolas's mother
sharply.

"But he calls you occasionally?"

"Yes, occasionally."

"If he calls, then, would you let him know? The problem
is, if he doesn't come today, he might get too far away . . . You
have no idea what his itinerary is?"

"No. I'm so sorry."

"Well, all right," said the teacher. "Would you like to talk to Nicolas?"

"Thank you."

The teacher handed the receiver to Nicolas and went out into the hallway to give him privacy. Nicolas and his mother didn't know what to say to each other. As far as his bag was concerned, there was nothing more to be said; all they could do was wait for his father to bring it back to the chalet. Nicolas didn't want to complain or cause his mother any further worry, while she didn't want to ask questions that would increase a distress she had no means of alleviating. So she simply urged him to behave himself and do as he was told, the same advice she would have given him if nothing had been wrong. Nicolas had the bitter impression that if she saw him halfway down the throat of a crocodile she'd still keep saying, Have a nice time, be good, don't forget to dress warmly . . . As for dressing warmly, she could hardly say that now and was probably being careful not to remind him to wear the big sweater with the reindeer on it that she'd knitted for him.

Accompanying the teacher back downstairs to the main room, where the breakfast tables were being cleared, Nicolas pondered the mystery: he knew his bag was in the trunk of the car—he'd seen it wedged between the tire chains and the sample cases—and his father could not have failed to notice it when opening the trunk, which he'd certainly had to do last night or this morning, at the latest, when he called on his clients. So why hadn't he phoned? Why hadn't he shown up? He must have had some idea of the trouble he was causing Nicolas. Had he lost the phone number of the chalet? Or the keys to the trunk? Had they been stolen? Had the car been stolen? Or . . . had there been an accident? All of a sudden, this hypothesis, which Nicolas hadn't yet considered, seemed all too likely to him. To let him down like this, his father would have to be unable to come, unable to telephone. Perhaps the car had skidded on a patch of black ice, crashed into a tree, and his father was dying, his chest crushed by the steering wheel. His last conscious thought, the words he'd stammered to the uncomprehending rescuers, must have been, "Nicolas's bag! Take Nicolas's bag back to him!"

Imagining this, Nicolas felt his eyes fill with tears, and a great tenderness came over him. He didn't want it to be true, of course, but at the same time he would have liked to appear before the others in the role of an orphan, the hero of a tragedy. They would try to console him, Hodkann would want to comfort him, and he would be inconsolable. He wondered if the teacher had reached the same conclusion and was trying to conceal her alarm from him as long as some hope still remained. Probably not. Not yet. Nicolas envisioned the moment when the phone would ring. The teacher would calmly go upstairs to answer it; the children would be carrying on in the main room, making a racket. He alone would be on the alert, awaiting her return. And there she was, her face pale and drawn. The children kept up the commotion but she didn't order them to be quiet. She seemed to hear nothing, to notice nothing, to see only Nicolas as she came toward him, reached for his hand, led him away to the office. She closed the door behind her, shutting out the noise from downstairs. She took his face between her hands, gently, the palms cradling his cheeks; you could see her lips trembling, and she said falteringly, "Nicolas . . . Listen, Nicolas, you're going to have to be very brave . . ." Then they would both begin to cry, she would be hugging him, and it was sweet, incredibly sweet—he would have liked that moment to last all his life, to fill his whole life, leaving room for nothing else, no other face, no other perfume, no other words, only his name repeated softly, Nicolas, Nicolas, nothing more.

10

BEFORE THEY LEFT, THE TEACHER AND THE INSTRUCTORS made more coffee while they discussed what to do about Nicolas. He had remained with them, apart from the other children, having apparently settled into his role as a problem to be solved.

"Listen," said Patrick, "there's no need to agonize over this. If it turns out that his father has completely forgotten about the bag, that he's a hundred miles away, then if we wait for him to come back, it'll spoil the kid's stay here and everyone else's too. I suggest we take some petty cash and get him the basics, so that he can participate in everything like the others. Okay with you, little guy?" he added, turning toward Nicolas.

It was okay with him, and the teacher approved as well.

After lunch, during the rest hour when everyone was supposed to nap or read, Nicolas went outside with Patrick. The air was mild; sunlight glittered through bare tree branches. Since he hadn't seen any other vehicle parked on the muddy driveway in front of the chalet, Nicolas thought that they would get to the village in the bus and that the driver would feel strange about having only two passengers. But Patrick walked past the bus, which sat there like a sleepy dragon, and continued down the chalet's little service road for about a hundred yards. Slightly off to one side was a yellow Renault 4L, which Nicolas hadn't noticed when he'd arrived. "The carriage is here!" exclaimed Patrick, opening the door on the driver's side. He got in and slipped off his neck a long leather lanyard with the ignition key on it. Nicolas made as if to get in the back, but Patrick leaned across the front seat to open the door on the passenger's side.

"Whoa, there!" he said merrily. "I'm not your chauffeur!" Nicolas hesitated: he had always been strictly forbidden to ride up front in a car—his father wasn't one to break the law. "Get a move on, buddy!" Nicolas climbed in. "Anyway," remarked Patrick, "it's a pigsty back there." Nicolas peered at the backseat timidly, as if scared that a big dog hiding under the ragged plaid blanket was going to leap at his throat. There were some old cardboard boxes, a backpack, a small carrying case full of cassettes, a coil of rope, and some metal objects that must have been climbing gear.

"Better fasten your seat belt," said Patrick, turning the key in the ignition. The engine coughed. Patrick tried again, kept trying . . . Nothing. Nicolas was afraid Patrick would become cross, but he simply made a silly face and explained to Nicolas, "Patience. She's like that. You have to ask her nicely." Turning the key again, he pressed very lightly on the accelerator, and raising the other foot, he murmured, "Here we go, here we go . . . Good girl!" Nicolas couldn't hold back a little burble of excitement when the car started up and began rolling down the narrow switchback road.

"You like music?" asked Patrick.

Nicolas didn't know what to say. He'd never asked himself that question. They never listened to music at home, they didn't even have a record player, and everyone at school considered the music class a drag. The teacher, Monsieur Ribotton, made them do musical dictation exercises: he played notes on the piano for them to mark down on printed staves in special notebooks. Nicolas never got the notes right. He preferred the short biographies of great musicians Monsieur Ribotton dictated to the class, because at least they were in words, with letters he knew how to write. Monsieur Ribotton was a short man with a very large head, and although his pupils cringed before his violent temper, which had even led him—according to school legend—to throw a stool in a child's face, they thought he was ridiculous. They could tell that the other teachers didn't think much of him, that no one did. His son, Maxime, a sneaky, sweaty little dunce who wanted to be a police detective when he grew up, was in the same class as Nicolas, who didn't much like him but felt sorry for him anyway. One day, a boy sitting in the first row had stretched out his legs and accidentally dirtied the cuffs of Monsieur Ribotton's pants with the soles of his shoes. The teacher had flown into an enormous rage that had inspired neither fear nor respect, only contemptuous pity. With bitter, plaintive fury, he had announced that he was fed up with coming to school just so that someone could get his pants filthy, that he could scarcely afford them as it was, that everything was expensive, that his salary was pitiful, and that if the parents of the student who'd just dirtied his cuffs had enough money to pay for dry cleaning every day, good for them, but as for him, he didn't. His quavering voice made it seem as though he was about to burst into tears, and Nicolas had felt like crying, too, because of Maxime Ribotton, who had to endure the spectacle of his father humiliating himself in front of his classmates, shamelessly spewing out his appalling resentment at having been treated so cruelly by life. Nicolas hadn't dared look at Maxime, but afterward, during recess, he had been amazed to hear Maxime refer to the incident in a casual, joking way, assuring his listeners that they shouldn't be upset when his father threw a fit, that he calmed down pretty quickly. Nicolas had expected Maxime to leave the classroom without a word after that scene and never come back to school again. Then they would have heard that he'd fallen ill. A few kind children would have gone to visit him. Nicolas saw himself going along with them, choosing from among his own toys a present he could give to Maxime without hurting his feelings. He imagined the grateful look in the invalid's eyes, his wasted face and limbs racked with fever, but the gifts and friendly words would be to no avail. One day they would learn that Maxime Ribotton was dead. The band of good-hearted children would go to the funeral, and from then on it was to the grief-stricken father, old man Ribotton, that they resolved to be kind and to show their good hearts. They didn't behave rowdily in his classroom anymore or greet the names of the great musicians he pronounced so respectfully with idiotic rhymes: Stuck-in-the-dirt Schubert, for example, or Schumann the Moron.

Outside of those names, Nicolas didn't know anything about music, but rather than admit this to Patrick he answered evasively that yes, he liked it. He already dreaded the next question, which wasn't long in coming: "And what kind of music do you like?"

"Uh, Schumann . . ." he replied off the top of his head.

Both impressed and amused, Patrick grinned wryly and said that he didn't have that kind of music, just pop songs. He asked Nicolas to pick out a tape: all he had to do was get the little cassette case on the backseat and read the titles out loud. Nicolas did. He struggled to decipher the English words, but Patrick filled in the rest after the first stammered syllables and, at the third tape, said fine, that one would do. He slipped it into the tape deck and the music exploded, right in the middle of a song. The voice was hoarse, mocking; the guitars slashed like whips. There was a sense of brutality but of suppleness, too, like the lithe movements of a wild animal. On television, this type of music made his parents turn the sound down in distaste. Ordinarily, if anyone had asked his opinion, Nicolas would have said he didn't care for it—but that day he was thrilled. Next to him, Patrick was tapping out the rhythm on the steering wheel, moving in time to the beat, now and then humming along with the singer, joining in on an exuberant squeal precisely on cue. The car rolled along in perfect harmony with the music, speeding up when it did, sweeping through turns when the tempo slowed, and everything throbbed in unison: the tires gripping the winding road, the shifting gears, and most of all, Patrick himself, swaying gracefully as he drove, a smile on his lips, squinting against the sunshine glinting on the windshield. Nicolas had never heard anything as beautiful as that song. His whole body was caught up in it. If only his entire life could be like that, always traveling up in the front seat, listening to that kind of music. If only he could grow up to be like Patrick: as good a driver, just as relaxed, with the same free and easy way about him.

1 1

"OKAY," SAID PATRICK AS THEY ENTERED THE STORE, "TIME to get serious. What do you need?"

Only then, after the exhilaration of the car ride, did Nicolas remember what they'd come for, remember that his bag had been forgotten in the trunk of his father's car and that his father was probably dead.

"Can you tell me what was in your bag?" asked Patrick.

"Um, extra clothes," replied Nicolas, taken aback by the question. Patrick must have known what was in the bag because everyone had been asked to bring the same things. Each student had been allowed to bring along one or two items of his own choosing, though, like a book or a board game, and in Nicolas's case there had been the drawsheet recommended by the teacher in case he wet his bed. He didn't have the courage to mention this to Patrick.

"And also," he said thoughtfully, "I had my safe."

"Your safe?" exclaimed Patrick, astonished.

"Yes, a little safe, a present so I could keep secrets in it. There's a combination to open it and I'm the only one who knows it."

"And if you forget it, what happens?"

"Then I couldn't open it anymore. No one could ever open it again. But I know it by heart."

"But suppose you get bonked hard on the head and lose your memory? You've written it down somewhere, at least?"

"No. You're not supposed to. Besides, if I lose my memory, I wouldn't remember where I'd written it, either."

"True enough," admitted Patrick. "You're kinda clever, pal."

Nicolas hesitated, not daring to tell Patrick that actually there was a problem with the safe. His father had given it to him along with a closed envelope containing the printed combination, which his father had advised him to destroy after learning the numbers by heart. Nicolas had done that. But it had soon occurred to him that before giving him the envelope his father might have opened it, then skillfully resealed it, thus acquiring access to the safe. Perhaps he took a peek into it from time to time to find out what Nicolas was hiding from him. Perhaps that was the only reason he'd given it to him. Although Nicolas wasn't absolutely sure of this, he was wary and didn't keep anything more private than the gas station coupons in the safe. If Nicolas's father had opened it, he must have been disappointed. But it was more likely that he was dead. Nicolas wasn't certain, though, so he resisted the temptation to tell Patrick this and said instead, trying to sound casual, "I could give it to you, if you want—the combination, I mean."

Patrick shook his head. "No. You don't know me. I might just knock you out after you've told me and then go swipe your secrets."

"Anyway, they're in my father's car."

"I don't want to know. None of my business—the combination or what's in your safe." He grinned and, pretending to point a gun at Nicolas, demanded, "Whatcha got in the safe?"

"Nothing interesting," replied Nicolas glumly.

In the children's clothing section, Patrick picked out a thick woolen shirt and waterproof ski pants that Nicolas tried on in a dressing room while Patrick got together the rest of what was needed: two pairs of underpants, two T-shirts, two pairs of thick socks, one knit cap, and a toothbrush. The ski pants were his size but a bit too long. Patrick briskly rolled up the cuffs, saying they'd be fine, his mother could hem them later if she liked. Nicolas enjoyed this way of shopping, without spending hours hesitating between two styles, two colors,

two sizes, frowning with that anxiety entailed in every decision his parents made. He would also have liked a green-and-
purple jacket like Patrick's, but of course he didn't dare ask
for one.

Patrick chatted briefly with the clerk at the cash register
as he paid. She was a cheerful girl and it was immediately
obvious that she thought he was cute, that she liked his
ponytail, his long face and bright blue eyes, his effortless way
of moving and joking around. "This young man belong to
you?" she asked, pointing to Nicolas. Patrick answered no, but
if no one claimed him within a year and a day, he'd be glad
to keep him.

"We get along pretty well, the two of us," he added, and
Nicolas said the words over again to himself, proudly. He
wanted to tell the other kids, nonchalantly, that he got along
pretty well with Patrick. He looked down at his bracelet, the
one Patrick had given him, and promised himself that later,
when he was out from under his parents' thumb, he'd let his
hair grow into a ponytail.

Patrick put the music back on in the car, and while he was
driving, swaying to the beat, he made another memorable
pronouncement.

"So, doncha think we're kings of the road?"

It took Nicolas a few moments to understand what that
meant: everything was going well for them, they were having

a good time, there truly wasn't anything for them to worry about—and when he figured this out he felt a joyous exaltation, as though this were their own personal password, just between the two of them. He was afraid that his high-pitched voice would sound shrill when he spoke and betray his littleness, but he overcame this fear and managed to reply, as though it were of no particular importance to him, "That's right. We sure are kings of the road."

12

THE AFTERNOON SNACK WAS FOLLOWED BY PLAYTIME: charades, steal-the-bacon, make-believe. But that day Patrick announced that they were going to do something different.

"What?" they chorused.

"You'll see."

He told a group of them to push the tables, benches, and everything else cluttering the room back against the walls. He turned out all the lights except the ones in the front hall, so that everyone could still see. The children were excited by these mysterious preparations, stifling giggles as they pushed the furniture aside, guessing at what was to come—they were going to play ghosts or hold a table-turning séance . . .

Patrick clapped his hands for silence. "Now," he said, "you're going to lie down on the floor. On your backs." There was a bit more laughing and confusion as they all complied. Only Patrick remained standing, waiting patiently for everyone to find a place. In a calm, unhurried voice, he told them how to make themselves comfortable: first, stretch out, trying not to arch your back but keeping the whole spine flat against the floor; turn your palms up toward the ceiling; close your eyes. "Close your eyes," he repeated almost dreamily, as though he himself were closing his, settling himself to fall asleep.

There was a moment's silence, broken by an impatient voice: "What do we do now?"

"You don't get it?" someone called out. "He's hypnotizing us!"

Scattered snickers greeted this remark, which Patrick ignored. After a little while, he spoke again, as though he'd heard only the first question. "We do nothing . . . We're always busy doing something, thinking about something. Now we're doing nothing. We're trying not to think of anything. We're here, that's all. We're relaxing. Hanging out together . . ." His voice grew even more serene and soothing. He walked slowly around the room, through the maze of supine bodies. Nicolas could feel rather than hear that Patrick was passing close to him. He half opened his eyes but shut them immediately, afraid of getting caught.

"Breathe slowly," said Patrick. "Use your stomach. Make

your stomach go up and down like a balloon, but slowly, completely . . ." Several times in a row he repeated, "Breathe in . . . breathe out," and Nicolas sensed that all around, others were following along, joining in the rhythm. He thought he'd never be able to do it. When they had to blow into the balloon during the health checkup, he was always the one with the poorest lung capacity, and his chest felt as though it were in a vise that kept the air from circulating. He breathed in and out more rapidly than the others, in a raggedy way, gasping like a drowning person. Patrick went on speaking, however, in a voice that was strangely both more and more distant and more and more present. "Breathe in . . . breathe out," he was saying, and without understanding how, Nicolas suddenly found himself caught up in that communal respiration, a part of the wave that ebbed and flowed around him, enveloping him. He heard the other children's breathing and his own melting into it. His stomach gently rose and fell, obeying Patrick's voice. Inside him blossomed little hollows into which his breath was pouring the way the incoming tide fills the crevices of a rock.

"That's good," said Patrick after a moment. "Now you're going to think about your tongue." Somewhere in the room, a single child tittered. Nicolas reflected briefly that if everyone had laughed, he would have, too, and found it silly to think about one's tongue, but he went along with the others:

he thought about his tongue touching his palate, the way Patrick said it should; he felt its weight, consistency, texture—moist and smooth in some places, rough in others. This sensation grew quite peculiar. The tongue became enormous in his mouth, a huge sponge he was afraid might choke him, but just as the thought occurred to him, Patrick dispelled this fear by saying, "If your tongue becomes too big and bothers you, just swallow some saliva." Nicolas swallowed, and his tongue shrank back to its normal size. He still felt it, though; it was bizarrely present, as if he'd just become acquainted with it. Then Patrick told them to think about their noses, to follow the flow of air through their nostrils. Then to direct their attention behind their eyelids, between their eyebrows, to the backs of their necks. From there he went on to the arms, beginning with the fingers (which he made the boys uncurl one by one), moving up toward the elbows, then the shoulders. "Your arms are heavy," he said, "very heavy. So heavy they're sinking into the ground. Even if you wanted to, you wouldn't be able to lift them . . ." And Nicolas felt that it was true, he couldn't do it. He lay spread out on the flagstone floor like a puddle, while his mind floated over his inert body and yet inhabited it as if it were a house with deep foundations, exploring the passages running through his limbs, pushing open the doors of rooms that were dark, warm—above all, warm. Heat was now his strongest sensation, and he was not surprised to hear Patrick describe it, urging them to welcome it, enjoy it, let themselves be invaded by this intense but pleasurable warmth that flowed through their veins, swirled at the surface of their skin, provoking faint tinglings and longings to scratch that were best resisted. "But if you really want to," added Patrick, "go ahead, it doesn't matter." How did he know that? How was he able to describe these extraordinary things Nicolas was feeling—at the exact moment when he was feeling them? Was it the same for the other children? There was no more laughter, only placid breathing, attentive to Patrick's voice. All were visiting, like Nicolas, this mysterious territory within them, all listening with the same confidence to their guide. As long as Patrick was speaking, telling them where to go (now it was the legs, the individual toes, the calves, knees, and thighs), nothing could happen. They were safe, deep inside their bodies. It went on and on. How long had it been going on?

Suddenly, Nicolas sensed that Patrick was leaning over him. He heard a knee crack faintly. Patrick had crouched down, and he now placed his hands—palms quite flat—high up on Nicolas's chest, just below the shoulders, where they remained perfectly still. Nicolas's heart began to pound and his momentarily tranquil breathing grew panicky. He didn't dare open his eyes and gaze into Patrick's, looming above him. Very softly, Patrick whispered, "Shh," the way one quiets a nervous animal, and his palms weighed a touch more heavily on Nicolas's chest, the fingertips spreading out toward the shoulders so as to press them farther down, to thrust Nicolas even deeper into the ground. Nicolas felt as though he were panting, dashing around helter-skelter inside himself, bumping into walls, and at the same time he knew that none of this showed on the outside. His body remained motionless, tense in spite of Patrick's efforts, which Nicolas guessed were meant to help him relax. He could hear Patrick breathing quite calmly above him. He thought of the Shell stations' plastic model, of its thorax cover you could remove to look inside. Patrick was leaning on this cover, he was trying to identify, to tame what was underneath, but everything was in turmoil: it was as though all Nicolas's organs had fled in terror as far as they could from the wall against which pressed these firm, warm hands, and yet Nicolas would have liked these hands to stay there. He could hardly restrain a groan when they relaxed their pressure, then slowly withdrew. Patrick's knee cracked again when he stood up; the sound of his breathing grew fainter. Peeking through half-open eyelids, Nicolas turned his head slightly to see Patrick bending over another child, starting all over again. Nicolas closed his eyes. A sudden shiver ran through his body. Had his father taken the coupons out of the safe? Had he already gotten the plastic model when the accident occurred? Trying to calm down, Nicolas imagined once more how things would go: the telephone that would perhaps begin ringing now, while Patrick was silently pressing on someone else's chest; the rest of the evening, disrupted by the devastating news; then that night, the next day, his life as an orphan. All the same, he felt it wasn't right to let himself get caught up in such daydreams, which could bring bad luck. What if the telephone really did ring, if the things he'd imagined to make himself sad and console himself actually happened? It would be dreadful. Not only would he be an orphan, he'd be guilty, awfully guilty. It would be as though he'd killed his own father. One day, to illustrate his usual warnings about being careful, his father had told the story of a classmate who'd pointed a gun at a younger brother—all in fun, of course—without realizing that it was loaded. He'd pulled the trigger, and the bullet had struck his little brother in the heart. What happened next? wondered Nicolas. What did they do to him, this child murderer? They couldn't punish him; it wasn't his fault, and he'd already been punished enough. Comfort him, then? But how do you comfort a child who has done that? What can you say to him? Can you, can his parents hug him and tell him gently that it's all over, forgotten, that now everything will be fine? No. What, then? Try to lie to him so that his life won't be ru-

ined, invent a less horrible version of the accident, and gradually convince him of its truth? The gun went off all by itself,
he wasn't the one holding it, he had nothing to do with it . . .

"Very slowly," said Patrick, "you're going to start moving
again . . . First your feet. Swing them in circles around your
ankles . . . Like that . . . Nice and easy . . . You can open your
eyes now."

1 3

THAT NIGHT, NICOLAS WENT FOR A RIDE ON THE CATerpillar.

The grown-up who accompanied him wasn't his father but Patrick. They'd left his little brother with the father of the boy from the amusement park. Nicolas's brother was wearing his green slicker (with the hood up, even though it wasn't raining) and his red rubber boots. He waved good-bye to them while he held the hand of the other boy's father, who was still smiling. You couldn't see his face very clearly. Patrick had taken a seat way in the back of a car, with his knees resting against the metal sides, and Nicolas went to sit snugly between his long legs. The man in charge of the ride dropped the safety bar down across their laps and locked it in place.

The caterpillar started moving, gliding in front of the little brother still waving his hand, and then, rising abruptly, it left the ground. Up in the sky, the caterpillar hung motionless, then hurtled into its descent. Nicolas felt himself sucked into a void that was somehow inside him as well. His stomach turned over; he was scared, trying to laugh. Now the caterpillar was going fast. It came around to ground level again, whooshing like a speeding train, and shot immediately back up into the air. This time he barely had a chance to see the ticket window, his little brother, the people around him; he and Patrick were once more flung into the sky (but harder, faster), once more stopped at that frightening place and moment marking the sudden plunge down the other side. Nicolas pushed with his feet against the ground rushing up at them and held tight to the safety bar, while Patrick gripped it, too, his big, tanned hands clenched at either side of the small wrists. The sleeves of his sweatshirt were rolled up, revealing ropy veins that stood out prominently on his forearms. Against his back, Nicolas could feel Patrick's hard belly contract in apprehension on the edge of the abyss just as his own stomach did, and then tighten even more, trying to resist in that instant when their free fall actually began. There was a moment's respite at the bottom, but then they'd already begun the climb back, already reached the crest, and the marvelous panic of the descent was upon them again. With Patrick's taut thighs squeezing his legs, Nicolas kept his eyes tightly shut. Just before reaching the top, however, he suddenly opened them and saw the entire amusement park, far below: tiny figures, human ants milling about on the ground, light years away. During that brief instant, his eye was drawn to one—no, two—of these figures, a man walking away and a small child holding his hand. The caterpillar was already streaking earthward, it was impossible to see anything, but Nicolas realized what was happening. The next time around, he stared down, wide-eyed with icy horror; the man leading off his little brother was already farther away. They would be lost to sight when the caterpillar dove again, and at its next ascent Nicolas was certain that he wouldn't be able to spot them anymore. They would have vanished. He was seeing— had seen—his little brother for the last time, at least as he was now, with his eyes, all his limbs, all the organs in his body still intact. What had just slipped away before Nicolas's helpless gaze was the last image he would have of the child: a chubby little figure in a slicker and red rubber boots, holding the hand of a man in a denim jacket . . . and it was useless to cry out. Even Patrick (against whose body his own was pressed) would not hear him, and even if he did, even if he had seen the same thing, it wouldn't make any difference.

The ride lasted three minutes. There was no alarm button, and you couldn't get off once the ride had begun. For another minute and a half, two minutes, they were going to keep whirling around and around while his little brother disappeared behind a fence, led off by the man in the denim jacket to his accomplices in their white coats, and when the ride was over, when they'd climbed down unsteadily, it would be too late. Was Nicolas the only one who'd seen it? Or had Patrick, too? No, he hadn't seen a thing—it was better that way. When the ride stopped, he would lift Nicolas up from between his legs and clamber out of the car with a big grin, telling him again that they were kings of the road. For a few seconds longer he would remain unaware of what had happened, still able to smile. Nicolas envied him and would have given his life not to have opened his eyes, looked down, seen what he had seen, so that he might share Patrick's blissful ignorance and live one more minute with him in a world from which his little brother had not yet disappeared. He would have given his life to have that minute last forever, so that the caterpillar ride would never end. What had just happened, what was happening below would not exist. They would never learn about it. There would be nothing else on earth except the caterpillar turning faster and faster, the centrifugal force tossing them way up into the sky, pressing them tightly against each other, this hole gaping in his belly, sucking him up from the inside, filling itself for an instant only to open up again, going deeper and deeper, and Patrick's stomach against Nicolas's back, Patrick's thighs next to his legs, Patrick's breath against his neck, and the noise, and the void, and the sky.

14

THE DAMPNESS AWAKENED HIM, OVERWHELMING HIM with a feeling of disaster. The sheet was wet, as were the pants and top of his pajamas. Thinking he was back at home, he almost called out in tears but stifled his cry in time. Everyone was asleep. The wind whistled through the fir trees outside. Lying on his stomach, Nicolas was afraid to move. At first he hoped that the warmth of his body would dry the sheet and his pajamas before morning came. No one would notice anything the next day unless they climbed up to look, to sniff at the covers. But he didn't smell the characteristic odor of peepee. This smell was not as sharp, barely noticeable. The consistency of the puddle was different, too, like tacky glue between his body and the sheet. Worried, he stealthily slipped one hand beneath himself and felt something viscous. He wondered if his tummy had come open, letting this sticky liquid leak out. Blood? It was too dark to tell, but he imagined an enormous red stain spreading across the bed, across Hodkann's blue pajamas. At the slightest movement, his insides would spill out. A wound would have hurt him, though, and he didn't feel pain anywhere. He was scared. He didn't dare raise his hand to his face, bringing that gummy stuff, that jellyfish secretion from inside him, close to his mouth, his eyes, his nostrils. He could feel himself staring, his face grimacing with fright at the idea that something ghastly was happening to him that had never, ever happened to anyone else, something supernatural.

In the book of horror stories where he'd found "The Monkey's Paw," he'd read about a young man who drinks a strange elixir, then watches his body gradually decompose, liquefy into a blackish slime. He isn't really the one who sees this, in the story—it's his mother, who is astonished that he won't leave his room anymore, won't let anyone in, and speaks in a voice that becomes clotted, curdled, dropping lower and lower until soon it's a kind of incomprehensible gurgling. Then he gives up talking, communicates through notes slipped under the door, messages on which the writing deteriorates as well, the last ones little more than desperate scribbles on paper covered with oily black stains. And when—beside herself with worry—the mother has the door broken down, all that remains is a revolting puddle on the floor, at the surface of which float two lumps that once were eyes.

Nicolas had read this story eagerly but without any real feeling of terror, as though it couldn't happen to him, and now something like it was happening to him, now this gluey pus was oozing from his body. It was worse than a cut, it was a leak, something seeping out of him. Soon it would *be* him.

What would the others find in his bed in the morning?

He was afraid, afraid of them, afraid of himself. He had to run away, he thought, and hide, and dissolve off by himself, alone. It was all over for him. No one would ever see him again.

Cautiously, expecting every moment to hear a horrid slurping noise, he managed to lift his stomach off the sheet. Throwing back the covers, he crawled to the ladder and climbed down. Hodkann's eyes were closed. Nicolas tiptoed from the dormitory without waking anyone. Out in the hallway, the light switch gave off a tiny orange gleam but he didn't turn it on. At the very end of the hall, unobscured by shutters or curtains, the milky glow from the window overlooking the woods allowed him to orient himself. He went downstairs, his bare feet chilled by the tiles. On the second floor, all the doors were closed except the one to the small office where the teacher had called his mother that morning. He went in, spotted the telephone, and reflected that he could use it if he wanted. Talking quietly, in the dead of night, without anyone knowing—but to whom? It was also in this office that the teacher and the instructors kept all the notebooks of class records. He could have looked through them, hoping to find something about himself. On those rare occasions when he was left home alone, he used the opportunity to go through his parents' belongings, his mother's dressing table, the drawers of his father's desk, without knowing precisely what secret he was looking for but with the vague certainty that discovering it was a matter of life and death for him and that, if he did discover it, his parents mustn't ever find out. He was careful to put everything back exactly where it had been so they would not be suspicious. He dreaded not hearing the door creak when they came home, being caught, startled by his father's hand falling heavily on his shoulder. He felt shaky, and his heart raced with excitement.

He didn't linger in the office but went on down to the first floor. The pajamas were sticking to his thighs, his stomach. A phantom class was assembled in the dim light of the hall, après-ski boots lined up along the wall, jackets hanging on a row of hooks. The front door was closed, of course, but only with a bolt, which he simply slipped open. He pulled the heavy door silently inward and saw that outside everything was white.

15

THERE WAS SNOW ALL OVER. IT WAS STILL FALLING, THE flakes spinning delicately in the wind. Nicolas had never seen so much snow, and in the depths of despair he was filled with wonder. The frosty night air stung his half-naked chest, a striking change from the heat of the house sleeping behind him like a huge sated animal, its breath warm and even. Nicolas stood still for a moment on the threshold, caught a snowflake lightly in his hand, and went outside.

Thrusting his bare feet into the as yet unblemished snow, he crossed the top of the driveway. The bus looked like a drowsing animal, too, the chalet's cub, nestled against its flank, dozing with its big blank headlight eyes wide open. Walking past the bus, Nicolas followed a path to the snow-covered road, turning around several times to look at his footprints, which were deep and, above all, solitary, spectacularly solitary: he was alone out there that night, alone as he trudged through the snow with nothing on his feet, in damp pajamas, and no one knew it, and no one would ever see him again. In a few minutes, his tracks would have vanished.

Just after the first hairpin bend in the road, near where Patrick's car was parked, he stopped. He caught sight of a yellow light moving through the branches of the fir trees, down in the valley; then it disappeared. Probably the headlights of a car on the main road. Who was traveling at that late hour? Who, without knowing it, was sharing the silence and solitude of that night with him?

Upon leaving the house, Nicolas had intended to walk straight ahead until his strength gave out and he collapsed, but he was so cold that, almost unconsciously, he headed for Patrick's car as though it were a climber's hut. To reach it he had to wade through snow that was up to his knees. The door was unlocked. He climbed into the driver's seat and tucked his legs beneath him, trying to curl up in a ball in front of the steering wheel. When he touched the seat, it was already wet and freezing cold. He slid a hand between his skin and the waistband of his pajamas, but the viscous liquid had dried into a crust; the trickling he felt was only melting snow. Shivering, he cradled his hand down by his lower abdomen, between his navel and the thing he didn't like to mention because none of the names for it seemed like the real one to him: not *weewee*, which his parents used sometimes; nor *penis*, which he'd read in the medical dictionary; nor *dick*, which he'd heard at school. One day, in a corner of the playground, a classmate had gotten his thing out and shown Nicolas, for laughs, how it obeyed him. It stood up when he called to it, "Come on, Toto! Jump up, Toto!" Holding it between two fingers, he pulled it down like a lever, making it spring back against his belly. It had to have a name, though, a real name that Nicolas would learn later on.

He remembered the story of the Little Mermaid, which had been, with *Pinocchio*, one of his two favorite books when he was very young. There was a moment that had always had a strange effect on him, when the Little Mermaid, in love with the prince she has glimpsed during a storm at sea, dreams of becoming human so that he might fall in love with her. This is why she seeks a magic spell from the witch, who gives her a potion to make legs grow in the place of her fishtail—and takes the mermaid's voice in exchange. Now she must make the prince fall in love with a mute, and if she fails, if the prince has not declared his love to her at the end of three days, she will die. The part Nicolas liked best was when she had to spend the night alone on the beach after drinking the potion. She lay down on the sand with her fishtail covered with leaves and waited on the seashore beneath the distant, glittering stars for the metamorphosis to occur. There was a drawing in Nicolas's book that showed her like that, with long blond tresses hiding her breasts, and scales that began just below her navel. The drawing wasn't pretty, but you could imagine the incredible softness of her belly, beneath the fishtail. During the night, in pain, the Little Mermaid didn't dare look under the leaves, where what was still her was struggling with what she soon would be. It hurt, it hurt a great deal. She moaned softly, fearing to attract the attention of the fishermen who were chatting around their fire farther along the beach, mending their nets. Quite low, for herself alone, she tried to sing, so that she might hear her own voice one last time. When dawn came, she could tell that the battle was over, that the charm had done its work. She felt that there was something different under the leaves, that what she had been had become something else. She was afraid. Her soul was unbearably sad, and her voice had already died away in her throat. Slowly, feeling their way along, her hands moved down her body and there, below the navel, where ever since her birth the scales had begun, the silky skin continued. Nothing so affected Nicolas as this moment—quite brief in the book—which he could spend whole hours imagining, when the hands of the Little Mermaid first touched her legs. Curled up in his bed, the covers drawn snugly about him, he would play at being the Little Mermaid before he dropped off to sleep. He'd run his own hands along his thighs, along the soft skin on the inside of his thighs, skin so soft that the illusion was possible, that he could believe he was touching the Little Mermaid's thighs, calves, ankles, the graceful and so-slender ankles of the Little Mermaid, and together they would be drawn as if magnetized, the Little Mermaid and he, back up to the inside of the thighs, where hands were kept warm, and it was so sweet, so sad, this feeling, that he would have liked it to last forever and he always began to cry.

He was too cold now, he couldn't make the tears come, but it was even more like it was in the story. He wasn't home in bed but alone outdoors, beneath the cold and glistening stars, surrounded by cold and glistening snow, and far from every-one, far from any help, like the Little Mermaid who under-stood at dawn that she no longer belonged to the world of sea creatures and would never, ever belong to the world of men. She was alone, completely alone, with no other comfort but her own warmth and the softness of her belly, and she coiled herself around this core, seeking refuge. Her teeth were chat-tering and she was sobbing with grief and dismay, for she al-ready knew that she had lost everything and would have nothing in return. It would have cheered her to hear her own voice, but she no longer had a voice—that was gone, too, and Nicolas understood that the same fate awaited him as well. No one would ever hear his voice again. He would die of cold during the night. They'd find his body in the morning: blue, stiffened by a thin crust of frost, almost brittle. Patrick would probably be the one who discovered him. He would gather him up in his arms, lift him out of the car, and try to revive him with mouth-to-mouth resuscitation, but in vain. It would also be Patrick who would close his staring eyes, eyes filled with suffering and horror. It wouldn't be easy getting the frozen eyelids to go down, and everyone would be afraid to meet the terror-stricken gaze of the dead little boy, but Patrick would find a way. With the tips of his deft, tanned fingers he would know how to soften and gently close the eyelids, and his hands would linger on the now sightless face, a face forever at peace.

His parents would have to be told. The entire school would come to his funeral.

While he was imagining how the service would be (a comforting thought), a branch scraped the car's windshield, and fear gripped him once more. Fear not so much of an animal as of a murderer prowling around the chalet at night, ready to tear apart any child careless enough to wander away from its protection, its friendly slumbering warmth. Nicolas remembered the car, the headlights he'd seen on the road below, the traveler who alone was awake with him that night, and he remained on the alert for a noise, for the muffled crunch of a step in the snow. His hands were tucked away between his thighs, which trembled uncontrollably; one hand clutched that tiny thing without a name, and he wasn't crying, but his face was twisted in alarm. He opened his mouth to shout without making a sound, opened his eyes wide to make a mask of frightful anguish, so that those who found him would understand just from looking at him what he had suffered before dying a few yards away from them, in the snow and the darkness, while they were all fast asleep.

16

HE WASN'T EVEN AWARE THAT HIS WHOLE BODY WAS shivering gently. He hadn't fainted, but the thoughts couldn't circulate anymore through the slowly freezing channels of his brain. Sometimes his mind felt sluggish, like a lethargic fish rising from placid, inky depths, approaching the thin skin of ice that covered the surface and leaving behind, just before vanishing back into the darkness, a tiny trace, a blink, an instantaneously erased ripple of astonishment: so that's what dying was . . . Diving lazily like that, into torpor, icy coldness, deep down to the calm black place where soon there would be no more Nicolas, no more body to tremble, no more consolation to seek, no more anything. He no longer knew if his eyes were open or closed. He felt the steering wheel against his forehead but saw nothing, neither the car door nor the stretch of snowy road and the fir trees framed in the window. At some point, however, a beam of light struck his eyelids: it moved around, going in different directions. Nicolas thought fleetingly of the nocturnal traveler, then of a gigantic deep-sea fish swimming around him, enveloping him in its phosphorescent aura. He would have liked to sink down, farther and farther down with the fish into the great depths, to escape from the traveler, to avoid seeing his face. He almost screamed when the flashlight beam blinded him as the car door was opened. A dark form leaned in, bending over him, and he seemed to choke on his own cry. A hand touched him as a voice said, "Nicolas, Nicolas, what's the matter?" When he recognized that voice, his entire body relaxed: muscles, nerves, bones, thoughts—everything began to melt, to flow endlessly, like tears, while Patrick was gathering him up in his arms.

He must have opened his eyes again, because he remembered the car door hanging open behind them while Patrick carried him back up the drive. In his hurry to get him inside, Patrick had neglected to slam the door shut, and the image of that door sticking out from the side of the car like a broken fin had fixed itself in Nicolas's mind. Later on, to make him laugh, Patrick and Marie-Ange told him that while they were rubbing him, he talked constantly about that door, saying that they had to go back and shut it. They were wondering if he'd survive, and he—he was concerned only that the door shouldn't stay open all night out on the road.

Then there had been light, Patrick's face, and Marie-Ange's, and their voices saying his name over and over. Nicolas, Nicolas. He was with them: their warm hands were moving over his body, rubbing him, wrapping him up, and yet they were calling him as though he were lost in a forest and they were part of a search party to find him. He lay in the undergrowth, wounded, losing blood, and heard their anxious voices in the distance calling, "Nicolas, Nicolas, where are you, Nicolas?" But he couldn't answer them. Once, steps rustled in the leaves: they were passing close by him without realizing it, and he couldn't make himself heard—they were already moving away, going off to search in another part of the woods. Later, Patrick picked him up again and carried him upstairs. They laid him down, put heavy blankets over him, held his head up so that he could drink something quite hot, which made him make a face, but Marie-Ange's voice insisted, said that it was good, he had to drink up. The glass was tipped and the burning liquid poured down his throat. Feeling began to return to his body, which was shot through by great, long shivers of such amplitude that they became voluptuous. He undulated under the covers like a big fish flapping its tail in slow motion. He kept his eyes shut, had no idea where he'd been taken, knew only that it was a safe place, that he was warm, that they were looking after him, that Patrick had come to save him from death and had carried him in his arms to this warmth and this safety. The voices around him had dwindled to murmurs; some slightly scratchy material was rubbing against his mouth. His body kept trembling with long, slow, convulsive movements that went down to the soles of his feet, where they lingered as though desirous of going farther, of stretching him out even more. He was so small, tucked into one end of the bed, cuddled under the blanket as though he were in a cave, and the foot of the bed seemed infinitely far away, and higher too. It towered over him like a gigantic dune, rising way up into the sky and slanting down to vanish beneath his cheek. Down the vast slope of this dune rolled a black ball. It was only a small spot at first, when it left the summit, but as it descended it grew bigger and bigger, enormous, and Nicolas could tell that it would take up all the space, that there would be nothing left but it and that it would crush him. The humming sound it made grew louder as it came closer. Nicolas was scared but soon realized that he could make the black ball retreat whenever he liked, could suddenly send it all the way back to the top, condemned to a fresh descent that he would again be able to interrupt before he was smashed. *Just* before: all the pleasure lay in letting the black ball get as close as possible, in escaping from it at the very last moment.

1 7

HE FELT HOT, QUITE HOT, HUDDLED UNDER THE COVERS. He was awake, but he put off the moment of opening his eyes, wishing to prolong the heat, the comfort. The insides of his eyelids were orange. From somewhere in the chalet—a washing machine, perhaps, or maybe it was his own ears—came a faint, soothing hum. The wash was going around and around behind its little porthole, tumbling slowly in the scalding water. Nicolas's knees touched his chin; the hand clutching the covers was pressed against his lips—he could feel the dry warmth of the knuckles. Somewhere in the bed was his other hand, somewhere in the lazy, toasty depths where his body lay all curled up. When he finally opened his eyes, the light was warm too. The curtains had been drawn, but behind them the sun was shining so brightly that the room was bathed in an orange glow sprinkled with tiny dots of light. Recognizing the table, the lamp shade, Nicolas understood that they'd installed him in the office where the telephone was. He let out a feeble moan, to hear the sound of his voice, then groaned again, louder, to find out if there was anyone around. Out in the hall, footsteps approached. The teacher sat down on the edge of his bed. Putting a hand on his forehead, she asked him softly if he felt better, if he hurt anywhere. She offered to open the windows, and the sunshine streamed gaily into the room. Then she went to get a thermometer. Did Nicolas know how to take his own temperature? He nodded. She handed him the thermometer, which vanished into the bed. Fumbling under the covers, still curled up in a ball, he pulled down his pajama pants and guided the thermometer between his buttocks. It felt cold and he had trouble finding the hole, but he managed, nodding again when the teacher asked him if everything was okay. She continued to stroke his forehead while they waited; after a moment, there was a faint ringing under the blanket. The teacher said that was enough time, and the thermometer made its way back to her. "Almost a hundred and three degrees," she read. "You should rest." When she asked him if he wanted anything to eat, he said no; something to drink, then—he ought to have fluids for a temperature. Nicolas drank, then withdrew into the warmth, the sweet and fuzzy sluggishness of fever. He played some more with the

black ball. Later, the telephone awakened him. The teacher
arrived as quickly as if she had been standing right outside in
the hallway. She spoke for a few minutes in a low voice, smiling at Nicolas all the while, then hung up, sat on the edge of
his bed to have him take his temperature again, and gave him
more to drink. She asked him gently if he'd ever walked
around at night before without realizing what he was doing.
He said he didn't know, and she squeezed his hand as though
satisfied with his answer, which both surprised and relieved
him. Still later, he heard the bus rumbling out in the driveway, and in the front hall, his classmates returning with cheerful commotion from their skiing lesson. There were shouts,
trampling footsteps on the stairs, laughter. The teacher asked
everyone to quiet down because Nicolas was ill. He smiled,
closed his eyes again. He loved being sick, having a fever,
pushing back the big black ball just when it was about to flat-
ten him. He loved these strange sounds—cracklings,
buzzings—coming from outside or inside his body, he didn't
know which. He loved being taken care of, without any re-
sponsibilities besides swallowing a little medicine. He spent
a wonderful day, sometimes letting himself drift off into a
teeming, feverish drowsiness, sometimes enjoying lying
awake, absolutely still, listening to the bustling life of the
chalet without having to take part in it. He heard a tangle of
shrill voices downstairs at mealtime, plates being stacked,

merriment, the tongue-in-cheek scoldings of the teacher and instructors. The teacher came up to see him every hour, and Patrick came once too. He felt Nicolas's forehead, like the teacher did, and told him he was really something else. Nicolas would have liked to thank him for saving his life, but he was afraid that kings of the road didn't do such things, that it would sound fake, soppy, so he kept quiet. At nightfall, the teacher told Nicolas that she had to call his mother again. She'd already called her that morning, while he was asleep, and now she had to bring her up to date on how he was doing. He could speak to his mother if he wished. Nicolas gave a long, drawn-out sigh, indicating that he didn't feel up to it, and heard only what the teacher reported. That he had a high fever, that it was too bad, of course, poor thing, but that no, he didn't need to be sent home. And there wasn't anyone who could take him home, either. Then she talked about sleep-walking. She said cases like this were not uncommon, but it was surprising no one had noticed it until now. Nicolas could tell, from what the teacher said, that his mother was protest-ing: he had never walked in his sleep before. Nicolas was an-noyed by her insistence on defending him from this accusation, as though it were some shameful disease for which she might have been held accountable. He was quite content to have the teacher put the previous evening's events down to sleepwalking. That way, he didn't have to explain himself. It wasn't his fault, it wasn't a question of willpower. They would leave him alone. "I'd like to put Nicolas on the phone," said the teacher, hastening to add, after Nicolas looked at her imploringly, "but he's asleep right now." Nicolas flashed her a grateful smile before snuggling down into his bed again, wriggling his entire body, burying his face in the pillow and smiling, this time, all to himself.

1 8

NICOLAS SLEPT WELL, AND THE NEXT DAY WAS A
perfectly happy one. In the morning, Patrick came into the office and, with the complicitous grin of a fellow king of the
road, told him that he'd been monopolizing the teacher long
enough: with all the snow that had fallen, there was no question of her missing any more skiing, and since they weren't
going to leave him alone in the chalet, he'd be coming along
too. Nicolas was afraid he would have to go skiing and tried
to protest that he didn't feel well, but Patrick had already
begun getting him dressed by adding several layers of warm
clothing on top of his pajamas, an outfit that made him look,
exclaimed Patrick gleefully, like the Michelin tire man. An-
nouncing, "Last layer!" he plopped the pudgy figure down on
the bed and swaddled it in the blanket. When he finally

picked up the bundle, only Nicolas's eyes could be seen. Thus burdened, Patrick went downstairs and made a grand entrance into the main room, where breakfast had been cleared away and the children were getting ready to leave. "Here's a bag of dirty laundry!" joked Patrick, and Marie-Ange burst out laughing. The others crowded around them. In Patrick's arms, Nicolas felt as though he had climbed a tree to escape a pack of wolves. They could growl, slaver, claw the trunk all they liked—he was safe on the highest branch. He noticed that Hodkann was not among the encircling wolves but off on one side, reading, without seeming at all interested in what was happening. They had not spoken to each other for two days.

In the bus, Patrick arranged a kind of bed for him from two seats and a big pillow. Marie-Ange said that he was a real pasha and that Patrick was going to spoil him rotten if this kept up. Behind Nicolas, the others snickered a bit, but he pretended not to hear.

"And now, off to the bistro!" said Patrick when they'd arrived in the village. He picked Nicolas up again, still wrapped in his blanket, and carried him to the village café, which was at the foot of the ski slopes. Chatting with the café owner, a big man with a mustache, Patrick installed Nicolas comfortably on a banquette near the window, which overlooked— through a balcony with wooden balusters carved in the shape of fir trees—the modest hill where beginners had their lessons. The children were already putting on their skis and waving their poles around, and Marie-Ange and the teacher seemed overwhelmed. Nicolas was glad to have escaped all that. Patrick gave him a bunch of old comic books (not very interesting, but something to do) and asked what the gentleman would like to drink.

"Give him a mug of mulled wine," chuckled the owner. "That'll get him back on his feet in a hurry!"

Patrick ordered Nicolas a hot chocolate, ruffled his hair, and went outside, passing in front of the window to rejoin the group. They all turned toward him confidently, as though he alone could solve every problem—defective bindings, lost gloves, incorrectly buckled boots—and always with a joke and a smile.

Nicolas stayed in the café for the three hours the skiing lesson lasted. He was the only one there, aside from the owner, who readied the tables for lunch without paying him the slightest attention. Nicolas felt fine propped against his pillow, swathed in his blanket like a mummy. He had never felt so fine in his life. He hoped that his fever would last long enough so that everything would stay the same the next day, and the day after that, and all the other days of ski school. How many more were there? He'd already spent three days in the chalet, so there must be ten left. Ten days of being sick, excused from everything, carried around in blankets by

Patrick—it would be marvelous. He wondered how he could prolong his fever, which he could feel letting up already. His ears weren't buzzing anymore, and he had to make a real effort to shiver. Now and then he groaned weakly, as though he'd half fainted and were once again beyond the control of his conscious mind. Perhaps, now that he was supposed to be a sleepwalker, he might be able to go outside at night again, to stretch out his illness and keep everyone worried about him.

The business about sleepwalking had been a lucky thing for him. He'd been afraid of reproaches, but thanks to this explanation, no one had blamed him for anything or even expected anything of him. He was more to be pitied, actually. He was suffering from a mysterious illness: they didn't know when it might strike again or how to prevent it. Yes, it was really a lucky thing. The teacher would convince his parents in spite of their misgivings. Nicolas walks in his sleep, they'd whisper at home. Of course, they wouldn't say it in front of him; when a child is seriously ill, no one talks about it in front of him. How serious was it, being a sleepwalker? The benefits were clear, but were there any real drawbacks? He'd heard people say that it was extremely dangerous to awaken someone who was sleepwalking. But how was it dangerous? For whom? What could happen? Was there a risk the sleepwalker might die or else go crazy, try to strangle whoever had awakened him? If he did something bad—really awful—during a fit, would it be his fault? Certainly not. Another advantage of sleepwalking was how hard it was to expose a faker. To claim you have the flu, you have to have a fever, which can be checked, whereas if Nicolas were to start walking around every night with a vacant stare and his hands held out in front of him, people might suspect that he was pretending in order to make himself interesting or to have an excuse for doing forbidden things, but they could not accuse him of faking if there was the slightest doubt about it. Unless, of course, there were some special ways of finding out. Somewhat uneasily, Nicolas imagined his father opening the trunk of his car to produce a device with dials and needles, a helmet he would strap onto Nicolas's head, something that would prove irrefutably, if Nicolas got out of bed at night, that he was completely conscious, that he was responsible for his actions and was trying to fool everyone around him.

Ever since Nicolas had fallen ill, there had been no more mention of his father. The first day, they had expected him to return or at least to telephone. That seemed to go without saying, for they assumed he would open his trunk and find the bag there. But as he'd given no sign of life, they'd simply stopped counting on him and wondering when he would arrive. If this silence had meant he'd had an accident, as Nicolas had thought, they would have discovered him by the roadside during the last three days. His mother would have been informed, and therefore he'd have found out too. Even if it had been decided to put off telling him, he would definitely have sensed from the way people were acting that something serious had happened. But no. It was curious, this mystery—plus the fact that everyone had so quickly lost interest in it, no longer seemed to notice it. Even Nicolas, at a loss for explanations, had stopped puzzling over it. He hoped only that his father would not return, that ski school would continue the way it was, with every day like this one, and that his fever would last and last. He looked outside, through the fogged-up window and the carved fir trees. On the beginners' slope, Patrick had lined up poles for the children to zigzag around. Some could ski already, and they teased those who couldn't. Maxime Ribotton came down the hill on his backside. Nicolas was warm. He closed his eyes. He felt comfy.

19

THE POLICEMEN WORE NAVY-BLUE SWEATERS WITH leather shoulder patches but no coats or jackets, and Nicolas's first thought, as he sat bundled in his blanket, was that they must be terribly cold. When they'd pushed open the door, a chilly draft had swept into the café—you expected to see a flurry of snow following close on their heels. The owner had gone down into the cellar through a trap door behind the bar, and almost a minute went by before Nicolas decided it was up to him to greet the new arrivals. Under different circumstances, this role would have intimidated him, but his fever and especially the fact that he'd been declared a sleepwalker inspired him with the boldness of someone who feels forgiven in advance, unfettered by the consequences of his actions. From his corner, rather loudly, he called out, "Hello!"

Busy brushing snow from their boots, the policemen hadn't noticed him and now looked around to see where the voice had come from, as though expecting to find a parrot's cage hanging somewhere. For a moment Nicolas thought he'd become invisible. To help them, he wriggled a bit. The blanket fell down about his shoulders. Then both men spotted him at the same time, cozily ensconced near the misty window. They exchanged a quick, almost alarmed glance, and hurried over to him. In spite of the fever and the sleepwalking, Nicolas was afraid that he'd made a stupid mistake, that he'd just jumped into the lion's mouth, that perhaps these weren't real policemen. Standing there looming over him, they studied him wordlessly, then glanced at each other again. The taller of the two shook his head, and the other one finally spoke to Nicolas, asking him what he was doing there. Nicolas explained, but now that the brief alert he had provoked was over, his answer didn't really seem to interest them anymore.

"Okay, so you're not by yourself," concluded the taller man, relieved. At that moment, the café owner popped out of the trap door. The policemen joined him at the bar, abandoning Nicolas. Their manner was grave: a child had disappeared from the hamlet of Panossière, a couple of miles away. They'd been looking for him for the past two days, without success. Nicolas realized what the policemen had hoped for when they'd first seen him, and he thought that in a way they'd come pretty close: two days—that meant the child had disappeared right when he himself had almost vanished.

When he was younger, Nicolas had read the *Secret Seven* adventure series, and he remembered that some stories had begun like this: one of the child detectives, overhearing a grown-up conversation, would nose out a mystery, which the band would then solve. He imagined himself outpacing the official investigation, finding the lost little boy and taking him to the police station, explaining modestly that it hadn't been so difficult: simply thinking about it had done the trick, and then he'd been lucky, of course. Raising his voice to make himself heard and trying not to sound screechy, he asked how old the boy was. The policemen and the café owner turned toward him in surprise.

"Nine years old," replied one of the officers, "and his name is René. You haven't seen him, by any chance?"

"I don't know," said Nicolas. "Do you have a picture of him?"

The policeman seemed more and more astonished at Nicolas's interest in the inquiry, but he replied evenly that he happened to have some fliers that had just been printed up for distribution throughout the surrounding area. He pulled a bundle from a bag and showed one to Nicolas.

"Look familiar?"

The photo was in black and white, poorly reproduced. Still, you could tell that René had blond hair, a Dutch-boy cut, and glasses; his smile revealed a wide gap between his front teeth, unless it was simply that one of them was missing. The text stated that he had last been seen wearing a red jacket, beige velour pants, and new après-ski boots. Nicolas studied the flier for some time; he could feel the policeman watching him, intrigued, probably torn between irritation at this kid playing the big shot and awareness that they shouldn't overlook even a single lead. Nicolas made the pleasure last awhile, finally shaking his head and saying no, he hadn't seen him. The officer was going to take the flier back, but Nicolas offered to hang it up at the chalet where his class was staying. The man shrugged. "The way things are going for us, why not?" remarked his colleague, who was leaning back against the bar, and Nicolas got to keep his prize.

The café owner, clearly bored by all this concern, said that the boy must have run away from home for a few days, nothing really serious.

"Let's hope so," replied one of the officers. The other one, the man leaning on the bar, sighed.

"Fliers like this make me feel sick. Because here you're seeing just one of them, and there's still a good chance we'll find the kid. But back at the station we've got a bulletin board full of them, and some are from a few years back. Three years. Five years. Ten years. We looked, and then in the end, naturally, we had to stop looking. We haven't a clue where the kid is. The parents haven't a clue. Maybe they keep hoping—anyway, they think about it all the time. Can you imagine? How can you think about anything else after something like that?"

The policeman had been speaking in a subdued, toneless voice, staring at the photo and shaking his head as though he might start banging it against the counter at any moment. His colleague and the café owner seemed embarrassed by this show of feeling.

"You're right, it's hard," agreed the owner, attempting to change the subject, but the policeman kept shaking his head and talking.

"What can they tell themselves, the parents, huh? That their kid's dead? That he'd be better off dead? Or else that he's out there somewhere, alive, that he's older, bigger? You know, you see the description—the jackets, the boots, height three feet eight inches, weight sixty-eight pounds—and then you look at the date, it's seven years ago. The kid's been three feet eight inches tall and sixty-eight pounds for seven years. What's that supposed to mean?" The policeman almost burst into tears but regained his composure. He sighed deeply, as if emptying himself out, apologizing to the others, and then, in the tone of voice one might use to say, "It's finished, it's all over, don't get upset about it," he repeated softly, "Hell, what's that supposed to mean?"

20

NICOLAS'S TEMPERATURE HAD GONE DOWN, IN FACT HE wasn't sick anymore, but everything continued according to his wish, as though he was going to be feverish until the end of ski school, as though once this niche had been selected, it was more convenient to have him stay in it. The teacher and the instructors didn't even try to justify his quarantine by taking his temperature or giving him medicine. They seemed simply to have forgotten that he might have taken skiing lessons like the others, eaten at the table with them, slept in a dormitory. Anyone entering the small office that had been his room for two days now found him lying on the couch, nestled in his blanket, engrossed in a book (or daydreaming, more often than not), and whoever was using the phone or looking for some papers would smile and say a few pleasant words to him, as though he were a household pet or a much younger child. The door was left ajar. Sometimes a classmate would stick his head in, asking if he was all right, if he needed anything. These visits were brief, not unfriendly, but pointless. Hodkann did not come to see him.

The afternoon of the day the policemen had shown up at the café, Lucas poked his head around the door to say hi to Nicolas, who called him into the office and asked him for a favor: Nicolas wanted Hodkann to come up, he needed to talk to him. Lucas promised to tell him and left. From downstairs came the muffled thud of falling bodies: Patrick was giving the class an introductory lesson in karate.

Nicolas waited until that evening, in vain. Was it that Hodkann didn't want to come or that Lucas hadn't given him the message? Suppertime arrived, then bedtime. There was the usual din, which lasted awhile, then all was quiet. The teacher and the instructors had gotten into the habit of chatting while they sipped herbal tea and smoked a cigarette before going to bed; their voices floated up now from the main room, but the words were unintelligible. It was then that Hodkann came into the office.

He hadn't made a sound, and Nicolas was startled: before he'd had time to plan anything, Hodkann was standing in front of him in pajamas, with a grim look in his eye. His expression indicated that he wasn't used to being summoned like this by a mere pup and that he hoped he hadn't gone to all this bother for nothing. Hodkann waited without a word. It was up to Nicolas to speak first, but preferring to keep silent as well, he drew from under his pillow the flier about the missing boy, which he unfolded to show to Hodkann. The small bedside lamp shed a soft orange light around the room; there was an almost imperceptible hum, too, that must have been coming from the light bulb. They could still hear the placid murmur of grown-up voices downstairs, occasionally enlivened by Patrick's hearty laughter. Hodkann nonchalantly examined the flier Nicolas had handed him. They were engaged in a kind of duel that would be lost by whoever spoke first, and Nicolas realized that he should be the one.

"There were some policemen in the café this morning," he said. "They've been looking for him for two days."

"I know," replied Hodkann coldly. "We saw the flier in the village."

Nicolas was floored. He'd thought he was letting Hodkann in on a secret, and everyone knew it already. They must be talking about nothing else in the kids' rooms. He would have liked Hodkann to give him back the flier—it was his only advantage, the only valuable card he had to play, and he'd stupidly begun by giving it away. Now Hodkann was going to ask why he'd sent for him, what he had to say, and Nicolas had already told him everything. Hodkann's anger, his crushing contempt, would fall on Nicolas. Holding the flier, Hodkann stared at Nicolas with the same chilly wariness as before. He seemed capable of going on like that for hours, never tiring of the distress he caused his victim, and Nicolas realized that he'd never be able to stand the tension.

Then, in his unpredictable way, Hodkann changed his tactics. His expression softened, and he sat down familiarly on the edge of the bed, next to Nicolas, saying, "You've got a lead?" The wall of hostility had crumbled in an instant: Nicolas wasn't afraid anymore; on the contrary, he felt united with Hodkann in that trusting, whispering complicity he'd often dreamed about, the kind that bound together the members of the Secret Seven. At night, by the gleam of a flashlight, while everyone else was asleep, they were trying to solve a terrible mystery . . .

"The police think he just ran away from home for a few days," he began. "At least, they hope so . . ."

Hodkann smiled with affectionate irony, as if he knew his Nicolas well and could tell exactly where he was heading. "And you," he said pointedly, "you don't buy that." He glanced down at the flier still lying unfolded on his lap. "You don't think he looks like that kind of kid."

This idea hadn't occurred to Nicolas; he found it a flimsy one, but having nothing else to fall back on, he nodded in agreement. Hodkann had accepted his invitation to join in the search for René, to follow the trail of the mystery. Nicolas already envisioned the two of them discovering secret passages, exploring damp tunnels strewn with bones, and since they didn't have a single lead, there was no point in being picky. Then a thought struck Nicolas out of the blue, dazzling him. His father had told him never to breathe a word about it, never to betray the trust the clinic directors had placed in him, but Nicolas couldn't have cared less: Hodkann and René were worth it.

"There is one small possibility," he said hesitantly, "but . . ."

"Let's have it," demanded Hodkann, and Nicolas blurted out the story of the traffickers in human organs who kidnapped children to mutilate them. In his opinion, that's what had happened to René.

"And what makes you think so?" asked Hodkann. There wasn't a trace of skepticism in his voice, only the liveliest interest.

"You mustn't tell anyone," explained Nicolas, "but the night I went outside, I wasn't sleepwalking. I couldn't fall asleep at all, and then from the hall window, I saw a light out in the driveway. A man was walking around with a flashlight. That seemed weird to me, and I went down. I hid so he wouldn't see me and I followed him to a van parked on the road. It was a white van, exactly like the ones where they have their secret operating rooms. The man got in and drove off.

The headlights weren't on—he didn't even start the engine, just let the van begin rolling down the hill on its own, so there wouldn't be any noise. That seemed fishy to me, you know? I remembered that story about the organ traffickers and I figured they must be prowling around the chalet in case someone came out all by himself . . ."

"If that's true, you had a close shave," muttered Hodkann. He was hooked, Nicolas could tell. This new role was enjoyable: it had all come to Nicolas in a flash, he was improvising, but a whole story was already taking shape before him and everything that had happened during the last few days could be explained, beginning with his own illness. He recalled a book in which the detective also pretended to be sick, even delirious, in order to allay the suspicions of the criminals and keep a close eye on them. That's just what he'd been doing, too, for several days now. In the book, the detective's assistant—very resourceful but not quite as smart—continued the investigation on his own as best he could, thinking the detective was out of the game. In the end, admitting he'd been faking, the detective abandoned the masquerade, and it turned out that by staying in bed he'd come closer to solving the mystery than his assistant had by shadowing and interrogating everyone. Caught up in his story, Nicolas actually thought it plausible that he and Hodkann might play out similar roles, and even more astonishingly,

Hodkann seemed to go along with this as well. They both imagined the organ traffickers spying on the chalet (that huge store of fresh bodies, of livers, kidneys, eyes), waiting for a chance that never came and making up for it with a child from the neighboring village, little René, who'd had the misfortune to be discovered alone nearby. It all fit. Horribly, it all fit.

"But why shouldn't we tell anyone about this?" asked Hodkann, suddenly worried. "If it's true, it's very serious. We'd have to tell the police."

Nicolas looked him up and down. That night, it was Hodkann who was asking timid practical questions and he, Nicolas, who was silencing him with cryptic replies.

"They won't believe us," he said, lowering his voice still further to add, "and if they did, it would be worse. Because the organ traffickers have accomplices in the police force."

"How do you know that?" asked Hodkann.

"From my father," answered Nicolas firmly. "Because of his job, he knows lots of doctors." And as he spoke, forgetting that everything was based on a lie he had told, he had another idea: perhaps his father's absence was somehow involved. What if he'd spotted the traffickers? What if he'd really and truly tried to follow them? What if they'd taken him prisoner—or killed him? Although it was fairly shaky, he confided this hypothesis to Hodkann anyway and, to strengthen it, invented more details: absolutely nothing must be said about this, either, but his father was investigating on his own, without the knowledge of the police. Using his job as a cover and taking advantage of his connections in the hospital business, he was on the trail of the traffickers. That was why he'd come to this area, under the pretext of driving Nicolas to the chalet: his informants had tipped him off about the presence of the van where the secret operations were performed. The hunt was desperately dangerous. The quarry was a powerful, unscrupulous organization, and he was going up against them alone.

"Wait a minute," said Hodkann. "Your father's a detective?"

"No, no, but . . ."

Nicolas broke off, and this time he was the one to wear a look of grim determination, studying Hodkann as if gauging his ability to handle the whole story. Hodkann waited. Nicolas realized that Hodkann didn't doubt any of what Nicolas had already told him, and he pressed on, somewhat unnerved by his own words.

"He has a score to settle with them. Last year they kidnapped my little brother. He disappeared in an amusement park and was later found behind a fence. They'd taken out a kidney. Now do you understand?"

Hodkann understood. His expression was solemn.

"No one knows this," continued Nicolas. "You promise me you won't talk about it?"

Hodkann promised. Nicolas enjoyed the effect his tale was having on Hodkann. He'd envied the prestige the other boy had derived from his dead father—a man who'd died a violent death—and now he, too, had a daredevil father, an avenger running a thousand risks, embroiled in an intrigue from which he had little chance of escaping alive. At the same time, Nicolas wondered anxiously what would come of that night's crazy extravagance, the torrent of fantasies he couldn't take back now. If Hodkann talked, it would be a complete catastrophe.

"I was wrong to tell you that," he whispered. "Because now you're in danger too. They'll be targeting you."

Hodkann smiled, with that mixture of jauntiness and irony that made him irresistible, and said, "We're in the same boat." At that moment, they slipped back into their former roles: Hodkann was once again the big kid to whom the little one had wisely entrusted his perilous secrets, the protector who would look out for him, taking things in hand. They heard chairs scraping over the flagstones of the main room, then the teacher and the instructors coming upstairs. Hodkann placed a finger to his lips and dove under the bed. An instant later, the teacher looked in at the half-open door.

"Time to sleep, Nicolas, it's late."

Drowsily, Nicolas said okay and reached over to turn off the lamp.

"Everything's all right?" asked the teacher.

"Just fine," he replied.

"Good night, then." Back out in the hall, she turned off the light there as well. Her footsteps faded away; he heard a door creak, a faucet running.

"Perfect," whispered Hodkann, plopping down on the bed again near Nicolas. "Now we need to make our plan of action."

21

AS SOON AS THE BUS PULLED UP ON THE VILLAGE SQUARE, at the bottom of the slope where the skiing lessons were given, Nicolas could tell that something serious had happened. About ten people, men and women, were gathered in front of the café, and even from a distance, sorrow and rage were clearly visible in their faces. Unfriendly looks were directed at the bus as the driver parked it. Frowning, Patrick said he'd go see what was going on. The teacher told the children to stay in their seats. Those who had spent the entire ride from the chalet singing a funny song about summer camp fell silent of their own accord. Patrick went over to the group in front of the café. He had his back turned, with his ponytail streaming over the hood of his jacket, so the children couldn't see his face, only that of the man to whom he was talking, who answered angrily. Two women next to him joined in, one sobbing and shaking her fist. For a few minutes, Patrick just stood there, and no one said a word inside the bus. Since the defroster had stopped working when the engine was turned off, the windows were steaming up; the children wiped the glass clear with their hands or jacket sleeves to see what was happening. They usually fooled around like that, drawing pictures, writing words, but Nicolas realized he was trying not to, trying instead to make a clear circle representing nothing, as though everything risked being insulting to the people gathered outside, who seemed capable, if provoked by the slightest gesture, of tipping the bus over, burning it and all its passengers. Finally Patrick came back. He seemed troubled now, not as outraged as the villagers, but clearly upset. The teacher immediately went to meet him, to hear what he had to say without the children listening in. Then Hodkann broke the silence, voicing not a suspicion but a certainty they all more or less shared.

"René's dead."

He'd said "René," not "the missing boy," as if everyone knew him, as if he'd been one of them, and now Nicolas felt overwhelmed by the anguish that waiting had kept at bay. Patrick and the teacher got back on the bus. The teacher opened her mouth, but instead of speaking, she closed her eyes, bit her lips, and turned to Patrick, who gently laid a hand on her arm.

"There's no point in trying to hide it from you—something very serious has happened. Something awful. They found René, the boy who disappeared in Panossière, and he's dead. That's it." He sighed, to show how hard it had been for him to tell them.

"Someone killed him," said Hodkann from the back of the bus, and once again it was less a question than an affirmation.

"Yes," Patrick replied curtly. "Someone killed him."

"They don't know who?" asked Hodkann.

"No, they don't know who."

The teacher moved the handkerchief she held clenched in her fingers away from her lips and with great effort managed to speak. Her voice shook.

"I would assume," she quavered, "that some of you believe in God. So I think those of you who do should say a prayer. That would be good."

There was a long silence. No one dared move. The windows were so fogged up nobody could see outside anymore. Nicolas clasped his hands and tried to recite the Lord's Prayer silently to himself but he couldn't remember the words, not even the beginning. He seemed to hear, far away, his mother's voice pronouncing snatches of it that he was unable to repeat.

Once she'd taught catechism class. When they moved, that was the end of that, and she no longer made him and his little brother say their prayers at night. He pictured himself (but it was absolutely impossible: simply imagining the gestures frightened him) putting his hand in his jacket pocket, pulling out the flier he'd gotten from the policeman, unfolding it—oh, the rustling of the paper!—and looking at the photo of René. He wondered what he'd do with it in the hours, the days to come, wondered whether he'd risk getting it out, keeping it, putting it somewhere. If he'd had his little safe, he could have stashed it there, buried the whole thing, and then forgotten the combination. If someone found it in his pocket or caught him studying the photo, wouldn't that give away what Hodkann and he had played at the previous evening?

Their nighttime conversation and his own fibs now seemed to him like a crime, a shameful, monstrous participation in the crime that had actually taken place. He could see René's chubby cheeks, his pudding-bowl haircut, the gap between his front teeth or else the space where he'd lost one of them. He must have put it under his pillow and waited to see what the tooth fairy would bring. Behind his glasses, his eyes were filled with terror, the terror of a small boy over whom a stranger is bending—to kill him—and Nicolas could feel René's expression clinging to his own face, his mouth opening in an endless, soundless cry. He would almost have been relieved if a policeman had searched his pockets and found the flier that would give him away. A policeman—or René's father, crazed with grief, ready to kill in his turn and doubtless ready to kill him if he learned what Hodkann and he had been up to. Were René's parents there, in the crowd gathered in front of the café and now hidden behind the wall of misty windows? Were they all still there? What was Hodkann doing? Was he praying? Were the others all around them praying in that chapel of mist? Would there be an end to this silence, this horror that gripped them all and in which, unbeknownst to everyone, he was so deeply involved?

22

THERE WAS NO SKIING LESSON. THEY DROVE BACK TO THE chalet and tried to get through the rest of the day. Probably a time would come when they could return to normal life, think about something else, but each of them sensed that that moment was still far in the future and would not arrive during ski school. There was nothing they could do, however, except wait for it. As playing was out of the question, the teacher decided to assemble the class for a dictation exercise, followed by arithmetic problems. Since some time still remained before lunch and they were all expected to write at least one letter to their parents during their stay, she suggested that they set to it. But after passing out a few sheets of blank paper, she changed her mind. "No," she murmured, shaking her head. "It's not the right time."

Standing in the middle of the room clutching the packet of paper so fiercely that her knuckles turned white, she looked exhausted.

Hodkann chuckled nastily and called out, "Let's write a composition, then. About our happiest memory of ski school . . ."

"Enough, Hodkann!" exclaimed the teacher, and then she almost shouted it, "Enough!"

Hodkann was the only one of the children bold enough to speak, reflected Nicolas. It was as if the fact that he had lost his father had given him that right. Later, during lunch, when even the clatter of cutlery seemed muffled in cotton, Nicolas asked Patrick if they'd found René near the chalet. Patrick hesitated, then said no, he'd been found over a hundred miles away.

"That means one thing, at least," he added, "which is"— he hesitated again—"that the murderer isn't in this area anymore."

"It also means," continued the teacher, "that there's no reason to be afraid. It's terrible, it's awful, but it's over. You're not in any danger here."

Her voice broke on the last word; the tendons of her neck stuck out like taut strings. She looked around at the children sitting at their lunch, as though defying them to challenge this reassurance.

"But he must have been killed here," insisted Hodkann. "He didn't travel a hundred miles on his own."

"Listen, Hodkann," said the teacher, in a pleading tone edged with a kind of hatred, "I'd like us to stop talking about this. It happened, there's nothing we can do about it, we can't change a thing. I'm truly sorry that at your age you all should have had to cope with something like this, but we must stop talking about it. Simply stop. All right?"

Hodkann merely nodded, and the meal continued in silence. Afterward, some of the boys began to read or draw, while others gathered for a game of Authors. Those who wished to play hide-and-seek were told to stay indoors and under no circumstances to go outside.

"I thought we weren't in danger anymore," remarked Hodkann flippantly.

"That's enough, Hodkann!" yelled the teacher. "I asked you to be quiet, so if you can't manage that, go upstairs to your room, by yourself, and I don't want to see you again before supper!"

Hodkann went upstairs without arguing. Nicolas would have liked to go with him, so they could talk, but the teacher would never have allowed that, and besides, Nicolas wanted to avoid drawing attention to a compromising complicity between the two of them. At the moment, each was better off looking out for himself. Nicolas stayed in a corner, pretending to read a magazine. Whenever he turned a page, he thought he heard the flier crinkle in the pocket of his jacket, which he was still wearing on the pretext of feeling cold. Bundled up like that, he seemed to be waiting to be called away, never to return again. The little boy's body, lying broken on the snow, floated before his eyes. But perhaps there hadn't been any snow where he'd been found. Had the murderer killed him there or here? Even if the killer had won his trust with presents or promises, which was how they operated, these bad men Nicolas's parents had always warned him about, it was hardly likely that René would have let himself be driven so far away without protest. Living or dead, he must have made the journey in the trunk, and it was even worse to think that he'd still been alive. Shut up in the dark, not knowing where he was being taken.

Nicolas's father had once told him one of those hospital stories he brought back from his trips. A small boy was to have had a minor operation, but the anesthetist had made a mistake, and the child had been left permanently blind, deaf, mute, and paralyzed. He must have come to in utter blackness. Hearing nothing, seeing nothing, feeling nothing with his fingertips. Buried in a slab of endless night. With no idea that people were hovering desperately around him. In a world that was close by but cut off forever from his own, the doctors and his parents peered in distress at his pasty face, not knowing if there was anyone behind those half-closed eyes who could feel and understand things. At first he must have thought that he'd been blindfolded, perhaps put in a body cast, that he was in a dark, quiet room, but that eventually someone would come to turn on the light, set him free. He must have trusted his parents to get him out of there. Time passed, though, impossible to measure, minutes or hours or days in silence and darkness. The child shrieked and couldn't even hear his own cry. At the core of this slow, unspeakable panic, his brain struggled to find the explanation. Buried alive? But he didn't even have an arm anymore to stretch out toward the coffin lid above him. Did he ever suspect the truth? And René, tied up in the trunk, did he guess what was happening? He felt the bumps in the road, he pitched around, bruising himself on the corner of a suitcase, touching an old blanket with his fingers. In his mind's eye, did he see the silhouette of the driver behind the wheel? Did he imagine that moment when, having parked in some isolated spot in the woods, the driver would get out, slam the car door, walk around to the trunk, open it? First a thin streak of light, which grows wider; a man's face bends over him, and then René knows with absolute certainty that the worst is about to begin and that nothing can save him. He remembers his happy childhood, the parents who loved him, his pals, the present the tooth fairy brought him when his front tooth fell out, and he understands that this life ends right there, with this atrocious reality that is more real than all that has come before. Everything that has already happened is only a dream, and here is the awakening, that cramped space in which he lies bound, the click of the key in the lock of the trunk, the glimmer of light revealing the face of the man who will kill him. That instant is his life, the sole reality of his life, and there is nothing left but screaming, screaming with all his might, a scream that no one will ever hear.

23

THE CHILDREN HAD THEIR AFTERNOON SNACK, AND THEN Patrick decided to have another session of relaxation. "To try to make your minds go blank," he said. But Nicolas couldn't make his go blank, and even with his eyes closed, he sensed that the others around him weren't managing it either. Lying on the floor, their limbs outstretched, they were all afraid of looking like the dead child. As before, Patrick spoke to them soothingly, telling them to empty themselves out, to feel heavy, heavy, to sink into the ground, to let themselves melt into it. One after the other, he named the parts of the body that were to grow heavy, but this time, simply hearing these words was upsetting, inspiring thoughts of being tortured. When Patrick mentioned their arms, calves, spines, the soles of their feet, a sensation of warmth in their fingertips, he spoke kindly and patiently, his voice enveloping them in tenderness, trying to reassure them, to tell them that all these pieces of themselves were friends, working together for their common good, but still the muscles would contract so that everything felt stiff, tight, tense, the way one is when besieged on all sides and even inside oneself. Patrick said to breathe calmly, deeply, evenly, to let the wave fill and empty the abdomen, ebbing and flowing, but their air was cut off, as it had been in the throat of the strangled child. Temples throbbed; fingers clutched at the floor. Ears buzzed with strange noises, difficult to identify: dull thumps, a clanking that probably came from the radiator near where Nicolas was lying but that also sounded like a car careening over a pothole or a "sleeping policeman," a speed bump in the road. Nicolas's father liked that expression, which made him laugh; it was one of the few things that did, the idea of driving over a policeman. The car jolted about inside Nicolas, in that dim, rough landscape, that treacherous terrain full of chasms in the depths of which sloshed liquids secreted by squishy glands with unknown names. The car made its way through his body, twisting as though on a winding road through those tepid, viscous things in his belly, crossing the pass of the diaphragm (where an almost unbearable weight pinned him down), climbing through the cavernous gorge of the lungs toward his throat, heading for his mouth: he was going to spit it out, with its horrid battered cargo in the trunk. Lying right next to the window, near the burning-hot radiator, Nicolas heard the engine rumble louder and louder, closer and closer. As it approached him, he could see the underside of the car the way you see it in a garage, when it goes up on the lift. All that rusty metal, blistered by overheating, was going to run him down, dribbling oil and blood over him just as a spider wraps its living prey in gluey secretions. Outside the window, tires squeaked on the snow. The engine stopped; one car door slammed, then another. Patrick said to keep going, to pay no attention, but they couldn't keep going: rubbing their eyes as though awakening from a nightmare, several children had already gotten up and gone to look out the window at the van parked in front. Now the police were knocking on the chalet door.

That's it, thought Nicolas: they're coming for me. He looked around for Hodkann, with the wild idea that they might flee together before they were captured, but then he remembered Hodkann had been sent to his room. By this time the teacher was greeting the policemen, ushering them upstairs to the little office that had been Nicolas's domain before his life had fallen apart. Then the teacher called to Patrick and Marie-Ange to come up as well, and Patrick made the children promise to keep quiet while they were on their own. No one would have dreamed of acting up. Each boy remained silently frozen in the pose he'd held since being surprised by the arrival of the van. They listened intently, hoping in vain to hear what was being discussed in the office, the door of which was closed to them for the first time since they'd arrived at the chalet.

"What do you expect they're saying?" someone finally asked, in a shaky voice.

"What do you think they're saying?" someone else replied disdainfully. "They're conducting their investigation!"

This exchange loosened their tongues. Maxime Ribotton announced self-importantly that his father supported the death penalty for sadists. A voice asked what that was, a sadist, and Maxime explained that it was what people were called who committed these kinds of crimes: raping and killing children. They were monsters. Nicolas didn't know what raping meant, and probably wasn't the only one, but he didn't dare ask and in any case guessed that it had something to do with the thing without a name, between his legs, that it was a kind of torture having to do with that—the worst of all, maybe having it cut or torn off. He was impressed by the confidence with which Maxime, usually so apathetic, handled these questions. "Monsters!" the boy repeated, cackling, as though he and his father had one of these creatures in their power and were preparing, before lopping off his head, to give him a taste of his own medicine. In Hodkann's absence, he had come into his own as a kind of star, talking in a loud voice, telling other stories about children who'd been abducted, raped, murdered, stories he'd read in his father's newspaper, a special one devoted entirely—if Maxime was to be believed—to that. The "bad men" spoken of in Nicolas's home (with an agonized but evasive insistence that never spelled out in what way, exactly, they were bad) seemed to be, more than Schubert, Schumann, and dirtied trousers, the main topic of conversation in the Ribotton household, and now that the topic had finally come up, Maxime the sullen dunce was in his element.

During this discussion, Nicolas was off by himself near the door to the hall, where he was suddenly startled to see Hodkann rush down the stairs and over to the front door. Their eyes met: there was something imperious in Hodkann's look, as though his life—and even more—depended on Nicolas's discretion. Without a sound, he slipped out of the chalet. Only Nicolas had seen him go. At the instant Hodkann closed the front door behind him, the office door opened. The policemen, the teacher, and the instructors could be heard as they now descended the stairs. Ribotton and the others stopped talking.

"This kind of investigation," sighed one of the policemen, "is complicated and time-consuming. You look and you look, you've no idea in what direction to move, and when you find something, most of the time it's because the guy panicked and slipped up." The five adults all seemed worn out. They glanced into the room where the boys, now hushed, were waiting, and the other policeman, the one who had spoken about missing children with such helpless anger in the café, shook his head again and muttered, "A kid that age . . . Holy Virgin, pray for us." Moved by the same thought, the teacher closed her eyes tightly; it was a tic she had developed since that morning. Then the policemen left. Nicolas and the others watched through the window as the police van negotiated the snowy parking area and headed down the tree-lined driveway to the road. No one used the drive except the occupants of the chalet, but the policemen put on their blinker anyway before they turned.

24

NICOLAS WAS THE ONLY ONE WHO HAD ANY IDEA
Hodkann was gone. He didn't know what he was scared of,
but he was terribly scared of whatever it was. Just the night
before, when they'd talked over what they called their plan
of action, Hodkann had thought (or pretended to think) that
he might be able to come up with some clue by carefully
searching the area around the chalet—even though three
feet of snow had fallen since René's disappearance—or by casually asking the villagers if they'd happened to notice any
strange vans around lately. A worried Nicolas had urged him
over and over to be careful. He would have preferred that
Hodkann not question anyone—even casually—and that, on
the pretext of pursuing their investigation, they simply continue each night their secret whispered conversation, made

thrilling by an impending danger that would have lost nothing in Nicolas's eyes by remaining make-believe. Now that the tragedy had occurred, what was Hodkann up to? What would happen if he hadn't returned in an hour? Or by tonight? If he disappeared too? If they found his dismembered body in the snow tomorrow? Nicolas would be guilty of having kept quiet. By speaking up in time, which meant immediately, he might be able to prevent the worst from happening.

It was growing dark out; the lights had been turned on. Nicolas hovered around Patrick, looking for an opportunity to talk to him privately, but every time he had a chance he hung back and let it slip away. It occurred to him that they might all of them be lured outside the chalet, one by one, each child going off alone in search of the one before, and in the end it would be he, Nicolas, who would find himself alone, truly alone, waiting until the man who had killed them all decided to come in and finish the job. Nicolas would watch the front-door latch slowly open—and it would be time to confront that nameless evil he'd always felt skulking around him and which was now closing in.

When they began setting the table for supper, the teacher remembered Hodkann off in his room and craned her head up the stairwell to shout that he could come down now. Nicolas shivered, but what happened was what he least expected: Hodkann strolled down and joined them as though he hadn't been out of his room all afternoon. When, how he'd gotten back inside—this Nicolas never found out.

Supper was eaten in an atmosphere of gloom that no one tried to dispel, after which they went to bed, earlier than usual. "Try to sleep well, guys," said Patrick. "Tomorrow is another day." Nicolas headed for what had become his room, but the teacher told him he wasn't sick anymore and could rejoin the others.

When he went to get his pajamas, left rolled up in a ball beneath the sofa cushion, he lingered for a moment in the office, which had ceased to be his special place ever since the policemen's visit. The soft light of the small lamp beneath its orange shade made him feel like crying. To hold back the tears, he bit down on his wrist, the one around which Patrick had tied the bracelet, now somewhat frayed. He thought once more about the day his family had moved, a year and a half earlier. The decision to leave the town where he'd spent his earliest childhood had been made very quickly, with a haste that had completely baffled him. His mother had kept telling him insistently, vehemently, that he would be much happier where they were going, that he'd make plenty of new friends there, but her agitation, her fits of anger and tears, her way of brushing aside, as though it were an enemy, the lusterless hair that would immediately fall back over her face like a curtain—these things made it almost impossible for Nicolas to believe her words of reassurance. He and his little brother had stopped going to school, and she kept them home all the time. Even during the day, the shutters remained closed. It was summertime: they stifled in a climate of calamity, siege, and secrecy. Nicolas and his little brother had asked for their father, but he'd gone on a long sales trip, she said; he would be joining them in the other town, in the new apartment. On the last day, when the boxes the movers would be coming for after their departure had all been packed, he'd sat in the middle of his empty room and cried the way you do when you're nine and something dreadful is happening that you just don't understand. His mother had wanted to take him in her arms to console him, repeating over and over, Nicolas, Nicolas, and he knew that she was hiding something from him, that he couldn't trust her. She had begun to cry, too, but since she wasn't telling him the truth, they couldn't even really cry together.

25

BEING BACK WITH THE OTHERS ALSO MADE THE SECRET
meeting Nicolas had to have with Hodkann more difficult.
Where had Hodkann gone, and to do what? With the teacher
keeping her eye on him, Hodkann hadn't broken the dismal
silence at the supper table and had gone to bed without even
brushing his teeth, without speaking to anyone, turning toward
the wall like a wild animal best left undisturbed. Stretched out
on the upper bunk, as still as a statue lying on a tomb, Nicolas
wondered if Hodkann was asleep or not. An hour passed like
this. Finally Hodkann whispered, "Nicolas," and slipping quietly from the bed, signaled him to follow. Nicolas climbed
down the ladder and tiptoed out to join him in the hall.

As Nicolas went by him, Lucas sat up suddenly, grunting,
"What are you up to?" But Hodkann stuck his head in the

door and simply hissed, "Shut up!" Lucas didn't need to be told twice. Just to be safe, they moved away from the bedroom, going over to the window at the end of the hallway. Hodkann hoisted himself easily onto the sill, sitting with his back to the casement. His silhouette stood out clearly against the black and white masses of fir trees drooping beneath their burden of snow, while his face remained in darkness. Nicolas was afraid of this darkness.

"So?" he murmured.

"Your father has a gray R25, right?" asked Hodkann tonelessly.

Nicolas realized that what felt so chilly on his forehead was what the horror stories he liked to read in secret called a cold sweat. He didn't reply.

"Yes," continued Hodkann, "it's a gray R25, I remember very well. When the policemen came this afternoon, I sneaked down from the bedroom and listened at the office door to what they were saying. They were talking about the things that were done to René, and I'd rather not tell you about it. It still makes me sick. And then they asked if anyone had seen a gray R25 in the area. The teachers said no—they must've not remembered, or maybe they didn't pay attention when your father was here. So I thought things over, and when I could tell they were about to leave, I came downstairs fast, ahead of them, and went to wait for them out on the road." After a brief pause, Hodkann added, "I told them everything."

He fell silent again. Nicolas didn't move. He stared at this face of darkness.

Then Hodkann's tone changed. Now he was trying to justify what he'd done without giving up any of his authority. "Listen, Nicolas," he whispered, "I had to. I know I promised you I wouldn't talk about it, but your father's in danger. That's obviously why they're looking for him, can't you see? The traffickers might be holding him prisoner right this minute. Maybe they've already killed him," he said with sudden brutality, as if to shake some sense into Nicolas. "But if they haven't, there's still time to find him, and we can't do that, not by running around looking for footprints in the snow. This isn't the Secret Seven, Nicolas—these guys are monsters. Nicolas, listen to me," he insisted, almost begging. "If there's any chance of saving your father and we let it go by, don't you think you'll feel bad about it for the rest of your life? If it's your fault he dies? Imagine your life after that."

Hodkann broke off, seeing that his argument was having no effect on Nicolas, who remained motionless. Hodkann gave up with a shrug. "Anyway, it's done." Then, slipping down from the window sill, he reached out to take Nicolas's hand. Sadly, softly, he murmured, "Nicolas . . ." Nicolas stepped back to avoid his touch. "Nicolas, I understand,"

Hodkann assured him, stroking his hair, trying to get Nicolas to lay his head on his shoulder, and this time Nicolas gave in. Standing pressed to Hodkann's chest while the other boy kept stroking his hair and quietly repeating his name, Nicolas felt the warmth of Hodkann's immense body, white and soft, as soft as an enormous pillow from which protruded only that hard, nameless thing jutting out against his belly. But Nicolas was tense, stiff, as though frozen in ice, while all was flaccid and empty between his legs. There was nothing there, a void, an absence. He stared over Hodkann's shoulder, out the window, at the dark mass of fir trees bending beneath the snow, and beyond, into the blackness.

26

THE NEXT MORNING, THEY FOUND NICOLAS HUDDLED beneath the open window, through which snowflakes swirled into the hall. He was awake, and his teeth were chattering, but he didn't say a word. Once again, as though he no longer had any other choice, Patrick carried him to the couch in the office. This time the teacher seemed more irritated than concerned. All right, Nicolas was a sleepwalker and you couldn't blame him for being upset after such a trying day, but she was upset, too, and worn out. She had no intention of going along on the big excursion Patrick had planned for the boys; she had hoped to get some rest, alone in the chalet, and could have done without having to take care of a sick and moody child. Since Nicolas clearly didn't seem able to be up and about, however, he was allowed to reclaim his place on the office couch for the time being, and the teacher retired to her room. The class left with Patrick and Marie-Ange. Only Nicolas and the teacher stayed behind.

Hours went by. Nicolas had pulled the covers over his face, and without moving, almost without feeling anything, he waited. He would have liked to experience once more the delicious warmth of a fever, his cocoon of obliviousness, but he wasn't feverish, just cold and scared. The teacher didn't bring him anything to drink or come to talk to him. There was no lunch. She was probably asleep. He didn't even know where her room was.

He must have been drowsing, too, because he was awakened by the telephone. It was already dark, but the others hadn't come back yet. The receiver jiggled slightly in its cradle. It rang for a long time. It stopped, then began again. The teacher came in, and telling Nicolas that he might perfectly well have answered it himself, she picked up the receiver. Her face looked sleepy, puffy, and her hair was mussed.

"Hello?" she said. "Yes, it's me . . . Yes, he's right here."

She glanced at Nicolas without smiling. Then she frowned.

"Why? Has something happened? . . . I see . . ."

She set the receiver down on the desk. "Would you mind leaving me alone for just a minute, please?" Nicolas got up and slowly left the room, keeping his eyes on her. "You should go downstairs, you'll be more comfortable," she added when he'd reached the hall, and she shut the door. Nicolas went as far as the stairs and sat down on the top step, hugging his knees to his chest. He heard nothing of what was being said in the office, but perhaps the teacher was simply listening silently to her caller. At one point he thought about standing up, tiptoeing over . . . but he didn't dare. When he leaned against the railing, the wood creaked sharply. A few yards away, a band of orange light gleamed beneath the office door. Nicolas thought he heard a muffled sound, as if someone was trying to stifle a sob. Although the conversation lasted a long time, he couldn't manage to hear anything else. Everything was drowned in a well of silence. Deep down, water glimmered darkly.

Finally he heard the receiver clatter softly into its cradle. The teacher did not come out of the office. She was probably standing in the same position, her hand still resting on the receiver; she was squeezing her eyes closed, trying not to scream. Or else she had lain down on the couch and was biting the pillow that still bore the imprint of Nicolas's head. A few days earlier, when he had imagined her learning over the phone about his father's accidental death, she had first sent him away, as she had just done, but afterward she had left the office, come toward him, taken him in her arms. She had wept over him, saying his name again and again. It was a wrenching scene, but a touching one, infinitely sweet, and now it could never take place. Now she was afraid to come out, afraid to see him, afraid to speak to him. She would have to come out, though—she couldn't stay in that office for the rest of her life. Cruelly, Nicolas imagined her distress, the unbearable anguish that had overwhelmed her after she'd hung up the phone. She was perfectly still; so was he. She must suspect that he was there, quite near, that he was waiting for her. If he were to knock on the door, she would call to him not to come in, not now, not yet . . . Perhaps she'd turn the key—yes, she'd lock herself in rather than show him her face and see his own. If he wanted, it would be easy to scare her. Simply speaking would be enough, out in the silent hall. Or humming. Humming something light, innocent, relentless, like a counting rhyme. She wouldn't be able to stand it, would start shrieking behind the door. But he didn't hum, didn't budge, didn't say a thing. It was up to her, not him, to take charge of the course of events, since events would have to follow their course. Gestures would have to be made, words spoken. Harmless words, at least, useful only for keeping up pretenses, for acting as if nothing had changed, as if the phone call had never taken place. Perhaps she was going to get out of it that way, by pretending it hadn't happened. By waiting for another phone call, waiting for someone else—someone braver—to answer it. It would be Patrick. The policeman who had phoned earlier wouldn't understand—he'd say that he'd already spoken to the teacher, told her all about it, but she would shake her head, close her eyes, swear in the face of all the evidence that someone else must have answered instead, someone pretending to be her.

It grew dark. Snow fell on the fir trees outside the window where Hodkann had spoken to Nicolas. There was noise downstairs. The class was back. Lights, shouts, hubbub. The long walk must have brought a glow to their cheeks, and for a few moments, perhaps, the class had forgotten the horror of the previous day. For them it was yesterday's horror, which would recede with each passing hour, soon fading into a memory their parents would take care not to revive. The mothers would speak of it among themselves in hushed voices, with knowing, pained expressions. But for Nicolas it would always, always be like it was now, at the top of the stairs, waiting until the teacher found the courage to come out.

On his way upstairs, Patrick found him sitting on the steps in the gloom of the hallway.

"What are you doing here, buddy?" he asked kindly. "You'd be better off in your office."

"The teacher's in there," mumbled Nicolas.

"Ah, really? And she doesn't want you around?" Patrick laughed and whispered, "She must be phoning her boyfriend!"

He knocked on the door, for form's sake, and as Nicolas had foreseen, the teacher asked, "Who is it?" in a strange voice. Since it was Patrick, she opened the door, but closed it immediately behind him. Now the two of them were holed up inside, thought Nicolas. Soon they'd all be in there, everyone but him, each one trying to shift onto someone else the burden of having to go see him and talk to him. To tell him the truth? No, they wouldn't be able to. No one could tell that truth to a little boy. Someone would have to, though. Nicolas waited, feeling almost curious.

Patrick stayed in the office for a long time, but he, at least, was brave enough to come out and sit on the steps next to Nicolas. When he took the boy's wrist to see what kind of shape the bracelet was in, his hands shook.

"It's holding up fairly well!" he said, and then, unnerved by the silence, he launched into some story about Mexican generals and Pancho Villa that Nicolas didn't understand at all, that he didn't try to understand, but that must have been meant to be funny because Patrick kept making these fake-sounding chuckles. He was talking for the sake of talking, doing his best, and Nicolas thought it was nice of him. If he could have, Nicolas would have interrupted him and said, looking him straight in the eye, that all this stuff about Pancho Villa was fine but not really necessary and that he wanted to learn the truth. Patrick could sense this and suddenly stopped telling his story, even though he wasn't anywhere near the end. Without trying to cover up his failure, he gulped like someone drowning and said very quickly, "Listen, Nicolas, there's a problem at home . . . It's too bad about ski school, but the teacher thinks—and so do I—that it would be best if you went home . . . Yes, that would be best," he added, just to say something, anything.

"When?" murmured Nicolas, as though that were the only thing he needed to know.

"Tomorrow morning," replied Patrick.

"Someone's going to come get me?"

Nicolas wondered whether or not he'd rather the police came for him.

"No," said Patrick. "I'm the one who's taking you. Is that okay? The two of us get along pretty well."

Grinning weakly, he ruffled Nicolas's hair; the boy bit his lips to keep from crying as he thought about the kings of the road. It must have been a relief to Patrick that Nicolas had questioned him only about practical details, not about the reasons behind their trip. Perhaps he found it peculiar that Nicolas didn't seem all that astonished. Still, the child did ask, in a barely audible voice, "Is it serious, what happened at home?"

Patrick thought a moment before replying, "Yes, I think it's serious. Your mother will tell you about it."

Nicolas began to descend the stairs with downcast eyes but Patrick held him back, squeezed his shoulder hard, and, trying to smile, said, "It'll be okay, Nicolas."

27

AT SUPPER, DURING WHICH THE TEACHER DID NOT appear, Maxime Ribotton (who didn't want to lose his new topic of conversation) started talking again about sadistic child killers and the things he and his father would like to see done to them. Patrick told him sharply to be quiet. Hunched over his plate, Nicolas ate the scalloped potatoes the cook had fixed to help the hikers get back their strength. To show their appreciation at the end of the meal, Patrick suggested that they all shout, "Hip, hip, hurrah!" three times, and Nicolas shouted along with the others.

Then he asked Patrick if he could sleep in the office on his last night. Patrick hesitated before giving his permission, and Nicolas understood that it was because of the telephone. He went upstairs to bed before the others did, without saying good-bye to them and without anyone noticing except Hodkann, who hadn't taken his eyes off him all evening. But Nicolas had never returned his gaze.

No one, apparently, was aware that he was leaving.

Fifteen minutes later, Patrick came up to see him and said they'd be hitting the road early the next morning. He should get a good night's rest. Did he want a pill to help him out? Nicolas said yes, swallowing it down with a sip of water. It was the first time he'd ever taken a sleeping pill. He knew you could die if you took too many at once. During the time when they moved and his father was gone for so long, Nicolas had looked all over for the bottle his father used, but he must have taken it with him, or else Nicolas's mother had locked it away in a drawer.

Patrick sat down on the edge of the bed, as if to talk to Nicolas, but couldn't find the words. No one would ever again be able to find any words to say to him. Patrick was reduced to the same meager gestures as before, the hand squeezing Nicolas's shoulder, the sad, affectionate little half-smile. Patrick didn't dare say "It'll be okay" again, probably sensing how hypocritical it would be. He sat quietly for a minute, then stood up. He had gathered together Nicolas's new things, the ones he'd bought for him at the store, and had put them in a plastic bag he placed at the foot of the bed, ready for the morning. He turned out the lights and left. Nicolas remembered his own bag, carefully packed a week earlier for his trip to ski school. The police must have found it in the car trunk, must certainly have searched through it. He wondered if they'd managed to open his little safe, and he wondered what they'd found there.

28

WHEN NICOLAS WOKE UP BEFORE DAWN, HE COULDN'T remember having fallen asleep. He didn't recognize his surroundings at first and thought he was in his own bedroom at home. He was afraid, because while he was asleep, they'd closed the door and turned out the light in the hall, breaking the promise they made to him every evening. He whimpered, "Mama," almost said it again louder, almost called out, but held back—and suddenly remembered everything. He lay for a moment without moving, hoping that the night would last forever. Those condemned to die must hope so too. His eyes grew used to the darkness, and he tried to think if there was anything hidden in the room that could help him in some way or another. That could stop the course of time, keep him out of reach, make him disappear. But he saw nothing. Hiding underneath the bed would be useless. Telephoning for help—but to whom? What would he say?

Going over to the window, he realized that it had bars on it. He had slept there for three nights without noticing them. Or had they just been installed, while he was asleep, to make sure he wouldn't escape? They seemed old, however, deeply embedded in the concrete. He just hadn't noticed them before.

No other way out except the door. He felt around inside the plastic bag, managed to put on his clothes. Getting into the jacket, he heard the familiar, sinister rustling of the flier with René's picture on it. He searched the desk drawers for money to help him run away but found nothing. Quietly, he opened the door and slipped out.

A light was on in the room below, faintly illuminating the top of the stairs, where once again Nicolas waited, motionless. Patrick and Marie-Ange were already up. They were talking quite softly, but the chalet was so quiet that Nicolas could hear them by leaning forward.

"One cube," said Marie-Ange, and a spoon clinked in a cup.

"Somehow," Patrick continued, "the kids will find out in no time. And then if the people in the village learn he's here, in the state they're in, you just can't tell what they'd be capable of doing."

"But it's not his fault," said Marie-Ange softly. She sighed heavily and murmured, "How awful, God, how awful . . ."

Nicolas heard a sob, then Patrick saying, "You know, it's atrocious what happened to René, but I think I feel even sorrier for him. Can you imagine having to deal with that? What kind of a life will he have?"

There was a silence; then Marie-Ange, still sobbing and stirring her spoon around, said, "It's a good thing it's you taking him back. You think you'll tell him?"

"No," replied Patrick in a hollow voice. "That—I just can't."

"Who will, then?"

"I don't know. His mother. She must have been expecting something like this to happen one day. His father already had some trouble, two years ago. It wasn't as bad, but still, it was ugly stuff."

More silence, sobbing; then, "I'm going to go wake him up. We have to leave."

Patrick found Nicolas standing at the top of the stairs, fully dressed, and tried to tell from his face whether he'd overheard them or not. But you couldn't tell a thing from Nicolas's face, and anyway, what difference did it make?

When they came back downstairs again, Marie-Ange set her cup on the table, dabbed at her red eyes with a wadded-up tissue, and, without a word, hugged Nicolas tightly. She also gave Patrick a little kiss, on the corner of his mouth, and then the two travelers left. It was still dark out. Everyone else was asleep in the chalet. Their feet sank into freshly fallen snow. Clouds of vapor puffed from their mouths, an almost opaque whiteness against the black of the fir trees. When they reached the car, Patrick asked Nicolas to hold his small travel kit while he brushed snow off the windows with his bare hands and wrestled with the wipers, which had frozen to the windshield. When he'd finished and had unlocked the car, Nicolas began to get into the front seat, where he'd ridden before, but Patrick said no. They were going to be driving on the highway, where police patrol cars watched out for such things.

29

"YOU WANT SOME MUSIC?" ASKED PATRICK. NICOLAS SAID he'd like that. Keeping one hand on the steering wheel, Patrick flipped through the cassettes in the carrying case. Nicolas wondered if he was going to play the same tape they'd listened to the day they'd gone shopping, but Patrick selected a different one, something slower and softer. Accompanied only by a guitar, the voice was almost plaintive, and even without understanding the English words, you could guess the song was about a winter journey on snowy roads edged with sleep. Nicolas stretched out on the backseat, using a frayed old blanket as a pillow. The blanket smelled of dog, and Nicolas almost asked Patrick if he had one at home, and where home was, and what it was like where he lived, but he didn't want to seem as if he was trying to make conversation, so he kept quiet. Patrick was probably dreading his questions, and Nicolas decided not to ask any. Since he was lying with his head behind the passenger's seat, he could look up and see Patrick concentrating on his driving. The end of his ponytail lay across one shoulder. Nicolas had noticed his hands on the steering wheel: tanned and muscular, exactly the hands that Nicolas would have liked to have when he grew up, but now he knew that was impossible. The heater was set on high, to keep the windows from fogging. Nicolas had curled up, tucking his hands between his thighs, and he realized to his astonishment that he could doze, allowing himself to be lulled to sleep—as though he were feverish—by the heat, the serene and wistful music, the soothing hum of the defroster. Before the drive to the chalet, he'd counted the miles on his father's map: two hundred and sixty. He and Patrick hadn't gone even fifteen yet. As long as he stayed inside the car, he was safe.

When he woke up, they were already on the highway. The snow was all gone, but the sky was white. Patrick hadn't put in another tape, probably to avoid disturbing Nicolas's sleep. He'd turned off the defroster. He was sitting up straight, concentrating on the road ahead, with his ponytail still draped over one shoulder as if he hadn't moved the whole time. Although he had certainly noticed when Nicolas sat up, Patrick hadn't said anything. Only after a few minutes did he force himself to ask, in what was meant to be a jolly tone, "Did you have a nice nap?" Nicolas answered yes, and then silence fell again. Nicolas kept an eye out for signs along the highway that would show how far it still was to the town where he lived. A hundred and twenty miles. They were almost halfway there. Nicolas reproached himself for having let the first half of the trip slip by so fast while he was asleep. He had the feeling that things would now start happening more and more quickly.

Patrick moved over into the right lane, slowed, and got off at an Esso station. Nicolas remembered Shell's prize coupons and suddenly began to cry, quietly, without sobbing. Tears trickled down his cheeks. Patrick would never have known if he hadn't stopped the car in front of the pumps at that instant and turned around. Nicolas couldn't stop weeping; he looked down, away from Patrick, who stayed twisted sideways in his seat for a moment, gazing at him without a word. "Nicolas," he sighed, one more time. That was the only thing left to do—say a name over and over, with love and despair. René's parents must have been doing that, too, at night, lying in the bed where they would never sleep peacefully, ever again—and the parents of the child buried alive by the botched anesthesia . . .

"Come on, Nicolas," said Patrick finally. "We'll have something to eat. You didn't have any breakfast, you must be hungry." Nicolas wasn't hungry and suspected Patrick wasn't either, but after the gas tank had been filled, he followed Patrick into the restaurant.

Near the entrance was a newspaper rack, before which Patrick had a moment of panic. He tried to distract Nicolas and block his view of it, but although Nicolas pretended not to notice, he still caught a glimpse of the photo and the word "fiend" in the headline half hidden by the fold in the newspaper. Patrick quickly dragged him over to the vending machine and made certain that they could leave by another door. He got himself a coffee, bought an orange juice and a *pain au chocolat* for Nicolas, then led him over to the corner by the rest rooms, where there were three gray plastic tables. They were sticky and cluttered with empty paper cups. Patrick politely said hello to the only person sitting there, a blond woman drinking coffee. She returned his greeting and gave Nicolas a smile that pierced him to the heart.

Her fur coat, which gleamed as if covered with dew, was open over a blue dress of some precious, shimmering material. The wisps of blond hair that had escaped from her loose chignon seemed to invite a caress. She stood out against the grimy drabness of the place with her air of wealth, luxury, and above all, gentleness—a gentleness that was enveloping, magical, almost unbearable. She was beautiful. Precious, gentle, and beautiful. She calmly surveyed her dreary surroundings and the parking lot outside, and when her gaze fell on Nicolas again, she smiled at him once more, with a smile that was neither distracted nor forced, but personally meant for him, bathing the whole of him in the celestial tenderness that surrounded her like a halo. Her blue silk dress, cut rather low, revealed the beginning of her breasts, and a bizarre thought struck Nicolas: everything inside her body—her internal organs, her intestines, the blood flowing in her veins—had to be as pristine and luminous as her smile. He remembered the Blue Fairy in *Pinocchio*. With her, there would be nothing more to fear. She could, if she wanted, make the horror disappear, make what had happened go away, and if she knew, she would want to, that was certain.

Patrick stood up, saying he was going to the bathroom for a minute. Nicolas realized that his fate would be decided in that minute. He had to speak to the fairy. Tell her to save him, to take him away with her to where she was going. He wouldn't have to explain; he was sure she'd understand. One sentence would be enough: "Please save me, take me with you." She would be astonished for a moment, but studying him attentively, with the care, the sweetness that touched your soul and made you want to cry, she would see that he was telling the truth, that only she could work the miracle. "Come," she would say, taking him by the hand. They would hurry to her car, leaving the highway at the next exit. They would drive a long time, sitting side by side. As she drove, she would smile at him, saying soothingly that it was over now. They would go far, far away, to where she lived a life as precious, gentle, and beautiful as she was, and she would let him stay with her always, out of danger, at peace.

Nicolas opened his mouth, but no sound came out. He had to attract her attention, to send her his message with his eyes, at least. She had to look at him, see his mute supplication—that would be enough: she would understand. Yes, yes, she would understand. She would know how to sense the anguish within a little boy encountered by chance at a rest stop, and she would know that she alone could set him free. But she wasn't looking at him anymore, she was looking outside, watching a man dressed in black who was striding toward them across the parking lot. Almost choking on the silence that caught in his throat, Nicolas saw the man come closer, push open the glass door. Bending a loving face over the woman, he kissed her on the neck, near the wisps of hair from her chignon. She smiled up at him with her heavenly smile. Now she had eyes only for him. Never in his life had Nicolas ever hated anyone so much, not even Hodkann.

"It's fixed," the man said. "We can go."

The fairy rose and left with him. As she closed the door behind her, she gave Nicolas a little wave, then turned away. The man slipped his arm around her shoulders to keep her warm, and Nicolas watched them walk to their car, drive off, disappear. Underneath the table his fingers were knotted to-gether, hopelessly entangled, and he saw a kind of red-and-blue string lying on the ground between his feet, among the empty sugar packets and the cigarette butts. The bracelet had fallen off. He tried to remember the wish he'd made when Patrick had tied it on him, a week earlier, but he couldn't. Per-haps he'd hesitated so long, trying to choose the one that would best protect him from life's endless dangers, that he'd never made any wish at all.

30

FOR THE REST OF THE TRIP, NICOLAS WONDERED WHAT his last words had been. A short reply to Patrick in the car, most likely. He'd decided not to speak, not ever again. It was the only protection he could think of just then: not one more word. They'd never get anything else out of him. He would become a block of silence, a smooth, slick surface that would repel unhappiness and misfortune. Others would speak to him if they liked, if they dared, and he wouldn't answer them. Wouldn't hear them. He wouldn't hear what his mother would tell him, whether it was the truth or lies; it would probably be lies. She would say that his father had had an accident during his sales trip, that for some reason or other they couldn't visit him in the hospital. Or else that he was dead but that they wouldn't be going to his funeral or to pay their respects at his grave. They'd move to yet another town, perhaps they'd change their name, hoping to elude the hostility and shame that would dog them from then on, but it would be no concern of his anymore: he was going to keep silent, forever.

When they reached the outskirts of the town, Patrick reread the address that had been written down for him on a scrap of paper and asked Nicolas if he knew how to get to his house. The boy didn't reply. Patrick asked again, trying to catch Nicolas's eye in the rearview mirror, but Nicolas looked away, and Patrick gave up. He stopped and got directions from a policeman. Then they drove through the neighborhood in the rain. When they arrived at the street where Nicolas lived, it went in the wrong direction, so Patrick had to go all the way around the block, but he found an empty space right in front of the door. It took him two tries to get the car lined up properly along the curb. He opened the door for Nicolas to get out, then reached for his hand, as though Nicolas were a little child, but didn't speak, didn't say his name. Patrick's face had lost all expression.

Realizing that Nicolas was not going to help him, Patrick checked the names over the mailboxes in the narrow entrance hall of the apartment building. They waited for the elevator without a word. The sliding doors closed with a hiss. Patrick hesitated for an unusually long time before pushing the button. He was still holding Nicolas's hand, holding it very tightly. In the smoked-glass mirror on the elevator wall, Nicolas saw that he was crying. The box enclosing them seemed to sink into the ground, then rose with a shudder. The cable creaked. Nicolas hoped that the elevator would stop between floors and that they would stay there for all eternity. Or else that once it got high enough, it would break loose, plunging into a dark well that would swallow them up.

Nicolas's floor was a long, windowless corridor lined with doors, and his was all the way at the end. The light switch cast a dim glow along the hall. Patrick didn't turn it on. They walked down the corridor together, quite slowly. Nicolas remembered what Patrick had said that morning. "What kind of a life will he have?" They reached the door, behind which not a sound could be heard. Patrick raised his hand, hesitated even longer than he had in the elevator, and finally rang the doorbell. Gently, he withdrew his other hand from the child's grasp. There was nothing more he could do for him now. The carpet inside the apartment muffled the sound of footsteps, but Nicolas knew that the door would open, that in an instant his life would begin, and that in this life, for him, there would be no forgiveness.